# The Billionaire Wo

# 3 Part Box Set

*Part 1: Private Island Affairs*

*Part 2: Mated on The Speedboat*

*Part 3: Property of The Alpha*

© Copyright 2015 - All rights reserved.

This document is geared towards providing exact and reliable information in regards to the topic and issue covered. The publication is sold with the idea that the publisher is not required to render accounting, officially permitted, or otherwise, qualified services. If advice is necessary, legal or professional, a practiced individual in the profession should be ordered.

- From a Declaration of Principles which was accepted and approved equally by a Committee of the American Bar Association and a Committee of Publishers and Associations.

In no way is it legal to reproduce, duplicate, or transmit any part of this document in either electronic means or in printed format. Recording of this publication is strictly prohibited and any storage of this document is not allowed unless with written permission from the publisher. All rights reserved.

The information provided herein is stated to be truthful and consistent, in that any liability, in terms of inattention or otherwise, by any usage or abuse of any policies, processes, or directions contained within is the solitary and utter responsibility of the recipient reader. Under no circumstances will any legal responsibility or blame be held against the publisher for any reparation, damages, or monetary loss due to the information herein, either directly or indirectly.

Respective authors own all copyrights not held by the publisher.

The information herein is offered for informational purposes solely, and is universal as so. The presentation of the information is without contract or any type of guarantee assurance.

The trademarks that are used are without any consent, and the publication of the trademark is without permission or backing by the trademark owner. All trademarks and brands within this book are for clarifying purposes only and are the owned by the owners themselves, not affiliated with this document.

# The Billionaire Wolf Paradise

*Part 1: Private Island Affairs*

## Table of Contents

Chapter One: Island Escape ............................................................................................ 5
Chapter Two: Surfer Boy ............................................................................................... 11
Chapter Three: Something in the Water ...................................................................... 19
Chapter Four: The Pack ................................................................................................. 26
Chapter Five: Division ................................................................................................... 30

# Chapter One: Island Escape

"How many bathing suits do you think I should bring with me?" Jane asked, picking up a bright orange suit and putting it back down on the bed for the third time.

"How about none of them because you are staying here with me."

David stretched dramatically over the foot of the bed, hanging with his head upside down off of the edge. Jane sighed and shook her head at him.

"I told you, I need to get away from here for a while."

She picked up the orange bathing suit again, evaluated it, and shoved it into her luggage. With a groan of effort, David flipped himself onto his belly so that he was still draped off of the edge of the bed but now able to look at her with his best version of puppy-dog eyes.

"Why?"

Jane folded a few more pieces of clothing and tucked them into the case, doing her best to fill in all of the corners so she would only have to deal with this one piece of luggage and her carry-on rather than trying to juggle several bags during her solo trek across the airport.

"I feel like I've hit some kind of wall. Maybe I'm having a quarter-life crisis. All I know is that things have been great for years, but that is just the problem. They've just been consistently, reliably, tediously great. I have the perfect career, the cute little starter house, even the animal equivalents of the two-point-two children."

"Which one is the point-two?" David asked.

"Hudson," Jane replied, gesturing at the large aquarium across the room where Hudson the bearded dragon looked back at them from his favorite flat rock.

"Ah. So what you are telling me is that you have everything you could want in life."

"Everything but a man to enjoy it with."

"You have me," David pouted.

Jane leaned down to take his face in her hands and smiled at him.

"You are not exactly my type," she said before straightening and looking back at her luggage.

"You aren't mine either," he retorted.

Jane laughed.

"Tell me about it," she pushed down on the multicolored assortment of clothes one more time, "They need to create luggage for curvy girls. The twiggy ones can fit like three bathing suits in the space I need for one. I don't feel that is fair."

She rolled up one more skirt and poked it down into a small gap along the side of the case. Finally satisfied the she had filled the single rolling suitcase to its absolute capacity, she flipped the top over and pressed it down with her upper body as she fought the zipper closed.

"Well, if you insist on leaving me for an entire week maybe your dramatic escape to the islands will at least result in finding a hunky surfer boy who desperately needs help oiling his…board. You may not need many clothes."

Jane flashed her devoted best friend a bright smile and dragged the suitcase off of the bed.

"From your lips, Honey."

"You'll be back Sunday night?" David asked, climbing off the bed and following her out of the bedroom.

"Yes. My flight gets in at eight. Don't forget to pick me up. I can deal with a cab to the airport, but it would be depressing to come home in one."

"It would. Can I bring balloons?"

"No."

"Confetti?"

"No."

"A sparkly sign that says 'Jane' in glitter?" David swept one palm through the air and gazed into the distance as if envisioning the glorious results.

"A sign will be fine. Ok, you know where all of the cat and dog food is, walk Alfred twice a day, the emergency numbers are on the refrigerator."

Jane scratched behind Alfred's ears and stroked her cat's back. David handed Jane her carry-on bag, turned her by her shoulders, and pushed her toward the door.

"We are going to make it, I promise. I'll take care of Alfred, Alfred will take care of Cleo, Cleo might try to eat Hudson, but I won't let her. Now, go. Flee to the islands. We have a steamy cat-dog-lizard rave planned for this evening and I need to cover the furniture in plastic and prepare the refreshments."

"That would be probably be much more amusing if I didn't have a little bit of concern that you may actually be serious."

Jane stepped out onto the porch and turned to give final instructions to David, but he shut the door and was grinning and waving at her through the front window before she could even get a word out. She took a steeling breath and strode to the waiting taxi, practicing her very best 'confident woman relaxing alone in the islands' smile with the driver who helped her load her luggage before driving off toward the airport.

Eight hours, two flight delays, and a wholly unpleasant taxi ride with a driver who seemed hell-bent on becoming the premier tour guide of the tiny island and circumvented the resort four times to show her the sites, that carefully practiced smile was long gone.

Jane slumped against the front desk of the resort, staring incredulously at the woman behind it. She knew that her makeup had long-since melted in the humidity and that her hairclip had given up the fight so that half of her hair dangled by her face in a study of surrealist sculpture, but that could not have mattered less to her at that moment.

"What do you mean someone else is in my villa?" she asked, doing her best to control her voice.

The woman clicked her long French manicured fingernails across the keyboard of her computer again, scanned the screen, and turned back to Jane.

"I'm sorry, Mrs. Michaels, but it looks like there was a booking mistake and the villa you selected is no longer available," the woman said coolly, her tone so smooth and dismissive it made Jane even angrier.

"It's Miss," she corrected through gritted teeth.

A vicious smile flickered over the woman's thin lips.

"Oh, my mistake. I didn't realize it was 'Miss'," she said with a smirk

That was it.

"Of course you realized it was 'Miss'. That is what is on my reservation. The one that you so brilliantly messed up, by the way," Jane exploded.

"Perhaps you should try one of the other hotels. Maybe something not so close to the beach."

The woman's eyes scanned Jane's body scathingly and Jane felt a creative string of choice words formulating in her mind when a well-dressed man stepped up beside the woman and held his hand behind her shoulders in the way that didn't make actually physical contact but said 'please walk away before you make this situation worse.'

"Thank you, Bitsy, I'll take it from here," he said in the soothing, even tone of a man accustomed to dealing with conflict.

"Oh, you have got to be kidding me," Jane muttered as Bitsy sulked away from the desk.

The man turned to Jane with a calming smile.

"I'm Clark Adams, the owner of the resort. How can I help you?"

"It seems that *Bitsy* gave my villa to someone else. The specific villa that I have had reserved for more than a month."

"Let me check this out and see if I can figure out what is going on. Can I have your name?" he said, turning to the computer and hitting a combination of keys that gave Jane the distinct impression that the clerk had not actually done anything when clicking around on the keyboard.

"Jane Michaels. Thank you."

"Absolutely. Well, that's strange. It looks like Bitsy accidentally upgraded someone from a standard room into your villa."

"Yes, I'm sure it was an accident," Jane said, cutting her eyes at Bitsy, who hovered in the back corner of the reception area purposely not making eye contact.

"Mmm-hmmm," Clark said as if this was not the first time luxury villas had miraculously become available for certain guests when Bitsy was manning the desk.

Jane leaned closer to him across the desk.

"You know, for someone who works at an island resort, she certainly is pale. Maybe she has a vitamin D deficiency. That could explain some of her attitude problem."

"I am inclined to agree with you," Clark said, still looking at the computer screen, "Ah. Good," he looked up at her, "It looks like we do have another villa available. It has been undergoing renovations, which is why it wasn't available for booking, but I can assure you it has the same layout and amenities as the one you originally selected. Would that be acceptable?"

Jane wanted to come up with a snarky reply, but Clark's kind voice and obvious aggravation at Bitsy had diffused the anger that bubbled up inside her. She nodded and the bob of her fallen hair in the corner of one eye reminded her of her disheveled appearance. Removing the clip completely, she shook her hair loose and then tried to pile it back on top of her head while scooting around the perimeter of the desk to catch up with Clark as he breezed past Bitsy and stepped out into the lobby. The bellhop who had been charged with handling her luggage as soon as she got out of the taxi still stood by the shining brass cart that looked somewhat pathetic with only her two pieces of luggage on it.

"Villa 13, please," Clark said to him and the young man grabbed hold of the cart and took off across the lobby toward the back door.

Still struggling with her hair, Jane followed.

"Go outside," she called over her shoulder toward Bitsy, who shot her a disgusted look.

Clark was apologizing again for the situation when she turned her attention back to him. They walked across the lobby and out the door that led onto a lushly landscaped path.

"This villa is a bit further out from the main building than your original one, but the seclusion makes it more peaceful, and it is the closest to some of the most beautiful areas of the island."

"I appreciate your help," Jane told him, stopping with him when he paused in the middle of the path.

"If there is nothing else I can do for you, I will leave you here. I have some, um, business to attend to back in the main building."

"I think I'll be fine. Thank you again for getting everything fixed for me. I've really been looking forward to this little escape."

"Well, I hope that it is as wonderful as you hoped from here on out."

"I hope so, too."

Clark nodded at her and turned, heading back the way they came. Jane made eye contact with the nervous-looking bellhop.

"Shall we?"

Without a word, he started pulling the cart down the path again.

"He's a nice man, isn't he?" The bellhop continued on silently. "Nice looking, too." Silence. "No? Not your type? More into the Bitsy look?" Still silent, but a quick look out of the corner of his eye. "No? Something a little more satisfying then?"

Redness was creeping along the bellhop's collar but he made a barely-audible grunt of agreement.

"Well, how about that."

They arrived at the door to the villa a moment later and the bellhop scurried to bring Jane's luggage inside then rush away. She laughed as she watched him, experiencing a fleeting moment of feeling bad for obviously making the young man uncomfortable with her teasing.

Her momentary regret dissipated quickly, however, when she saw the gorgeous man making his way around the side of her villa.

# Chapter Two: Surfer Boy

*Dear Lord, David the Gay Boy Wonder had had a vision.*

Since this was about as close to a religious experience as had ever come, Jane took a moment of silent reflection to appreciate its magnitude. As she reflected, however, she kept her eyes firmly affixed to the embodiment of David's hope for her as he crossed the path less than ten feet from where she stood. His skin was smooth and golden, stretching across muscles that looked specifically made for the beach. Low-slung blue and white board shorts showed off the chiseled V over his hipbones and a broad back that looked solid enough that she could probably use him as a boogie board.

Perhaps not.

She would be willing to test her hypothesis.

Just as the man stepped from the path and disappeared into palms, ferns, and tropical flowers that separated the villas from the beach, he glanced over at her and offered a dazzling smile. Realizing he was completely aware that she was staring at him, Jane smacked a hand to her forehead and turned to find refuge from her embarrassment in her villa. David must have been off on his vision because with that stunning first impression she would most definitely need every article of clothing she forced into that suitcase.


Lee had to turn around and take another look at the girl who was standing in front of the newly renovated villa. Growing up at the resort meant being witness to a never-ending flowing of waiflike girls in bikinis that left nothing to the imagination, not that there was much to think about in the first place. This girl was different. It was a nice departure to see a guest that actually made him look twice, and there was plenty for him to look at. The swell of her hips beneath her pink sundress was lush, the perfect complement to the dip of her waist that gave her body luscious curves and offered more than enough to hold. As he walked through the plants along the path and down onto the beach Lee found himself imagining what it would feel like to fill his hands with her.

Dropping his board to the sand, Lee dove into the water to cool himself. The waves crashed over him, but after a lifetime near the ocean he was not afraid of the water and didn't resist as it flowed over him and moved his body around as it pleased. After several minutes rolling through the waves and occasionally dipping beneath them to see what kinds of plants and animals he could discover in the clear blue depths, Lee swam back to shore and walked up onto the beach. He was enjoying the warm sand beneath his feet and the quiet solitude of this portion of the beach away from most of the villas when he saw Bitsy trying to run toward him.

Bitsy was not exactly what anyone would describe as an outdoors person and she never emerged from her apartment not wearing at least four-inch heels. The result was a struggling, staggering run made only more ungainly by the small box she held under one arm and the fluttering motion she did with her hand every time she tried to look dainty. Lee rolled his eyes and glanced back up in the direction of the villa where the new guest was staying. He was trying to figure out if he could make a run for it and disappear into the palms before Bitsy managed to make it all the way to him when he heard her voice coming over the sound of the waves.

It sounded somewhat like a strangled cry, but Lee figured it was her calling his name, which meant she definitely knew it was him and he would not be able to escape. He sighed with resignation and waved. Bitsy covered the last awkward stretch of the run and threw herself against him. The box tucked under her arm dug into his ribs and her dark-haired head slammed dramatically into his chest. Lee let out a breath and patted her upper arms.

"Hello, Bitsy. What is it now?"

Bitsy gave a sigh that sounded as though she carried the weight of the world on her shoulders, which was impressive considering her frame didn't hold the weight of a normal person much less anything else.

"Oh, Lee, it's your father."

"Isn't it always?"

She lifted her head to give him her best wounded look.

"He fired me," she whimpered.

"I'm sorry."

"That's it? Won't you talk to him?"

Lee was all too familiar with this routine from Bitsy. She'd had her designs on him for years and though she had been more than willing to amuse him in hopes that she could become the pampered and indulged wife of a young billionaire, he had quickly tired of her. As the daughter of one of Clark's oldest friends, however, it was not so difficult to just brush her off as he had girlfriends in the past. Now he viewed her in much the same way he did a mosquito: a small, aggravating, and unavoidable reality of the environment that must have some purpose in the greater plan for the universe, though he could not clearly identify it.

Fairly soon he learned to duck her when he could, be cordial to her when he couldn't, and appease her when he needed to in order to prevent problems for his father. Now that he had fired her, however, Lee might actually get a chance to deposit her neatly in his past and move forward. He just had to appease her this one last time so that he could get off of the beach before she got any ideas about his barely clothed body and the empty stretch of beach.

"Of course I will talk to him," he said, gently guiding her a step backwards.

He walked back over to his board, scooped it out of the sand, and started toward the path leading back to the main building. He wasn't really lying. He would definitely be talking to his father at some point that day. What they would talk about was just yet to be seen.

Knowing Bitsy always preferred others to fight her battles for her so she wouldn't follow him for fear she would have to confront Clark herself for whatever she had done now, Lee left her standing on the beach and crossed through the landscaping to the path. He slowed as he walked by the newly occupied villa. The sun was just starting to set and there were no lights on inside the villa. One window stood open, however, and the soft flutter of the curtains told him that the new guest had turned on the ceiling fan. He took as much time as he could to pass by the villa without making it look like he was purposely looking for her before speeding back up to get to the main building.

He crossed the lobby to the front desk where his father stood. Clark glanced up briefly before looking back at the computer screen.

"I really wish you would put clothes on before you come inside."

"I am wearing clothes."

"Actual clothes, Lee, and shoes. And preferably not with half the beach clinging to your surfboard."

"That would take all the fun out of it. Besides, the guests don't seem to mind." Lee looked over his shoulder and, sure enough, a group of sarong-clad teenagers was staring at him and whispering to each other. He looked back at Clark. "See?"

"Yes. However, I need you in your professional capacity right now and that does not include being in a wet bathing suit. Go put on something decent, I need you to talk to a guest."

"What's going on?" Lee asked, suddenly concerned.

Clark seemed unusually tense and even though Lee assumed it actually had little to do with what he was wearing and plenty to do with whatever the reason behind him suddenly firing Bitsy, he always felt nervous when his father was this stressed out. Ever since his wife died just a few years after they had finally achieved their life goal of building and running a successful resort on the island, Clark had been more withdrawn, tired, and strained. Lee had worked hard to live up to the reputation and expectations of his family's fortune, and managed to find exceptional success on his own, but he still felt like he was struggling to make his father happy again.

Especially when Clark's gaze turned toward the forest that lay just beyond the bounds of the resort and his eyes grew dark and worried.

Lee fought hard against that, too, but it was happening more often recently and Lee had a feeling it was only going to get worse as the summer drew to a close and the wave of tourists started making their way off of the island, bringing on the quiet and still that always tempted those that lived in the forest to come down for a visit.

"I had to fire Bitsy this evening," Clark told him, looking at him with exasperation in his eyes.

"I heard. She tracked me down on the beach to tell me and ask me to talk to you."

"Are you going to talk to me?"

"Isn't that what I'm doing right now?"

Clark paused for a beat as if contemplating what Lee had said.

"You aren't going to ask me to hire her back?"

"Definitely not. As far as I am concerned, the less of Bitsy around here, the better. She has been sniffing around me for way too long and I am really tired of it. Besides, she never was fantastic with the guests."

"Well, that is actually the problem. It turns out that she was really good with one guest, so good in fact that she gave him a villa that had been booked by someone else. Then when that guest confronted her about it, she was extremely rude and made a few thinly-veiled insults about her marital status and her weight," Clark gave a deep sigh, "but fortunately Ms. Michaels got in a few pretty good shots of her own. I stepped in before it went too far downhill."

"Ms. Michaels?"

"Yes, the new guest who was perturbed about her reservation being bumped."

"Perturbed?"

"That is putting it as politely as I can," Clark looked up at Lee and chuckled, "It was pretty great seeing somebody get the upper hand over Bitsy, though. Not many people can ruffle her."

"She was most certainly ruffled, I can tell you that," Lee answered with a smile. Suddenly realization struck him, "This Ms. Michaels, did you get her somewhere else to stay?"

"Fortunately one of the villas being renovated is finished and I was able to get her into that one. She will be kind of all alone at the end of the resort, but I assured her the amenities are the same and the surroundings are incomparable. She didn't seem too bothered by staying out there, but I want to make sure that she stays happy. I want you to pay her a visit, check in on her, reassure her that everything is settled and that we want to do whatever we can to make sure she has the best stay possible."

"The brochure treatment."

"Absolutely."

Lee glanced down at his board, brushing away some sand and trying to look casual.

"Is she in the villa at the very end?"

"Sand, Lee, sand. Come on."

"I'm sorry."

"Yes, she's in the last villa. How did you know?"

Lee shook his head. For some reason he didn't want to tell his father he had seen the enticing woman standing outside of the villa when he was crossing through the guest quarters on the way to the beach, and he definitely didn't want to tell him that he had lurked around outside that same villa hoping to catch another glimpse of her on his way to the main building.

"I heard George and some of the other guys talking about finishing up the renovations," he rushed through his falsified explanation and picked his board back up from where he had leaned it against the desk, "I'll go get a shower, get dressed, and head down there."

"One more thing, Lee."

Lee turned back to his father, already knowing what he was going to say. He could hear it in his voice.

"Yes?"

"Stay away from the forest tonight."

"Dad, you have heard the rumors. You know what might be happening – "

"Stay away from the forest," Clark cut him off, slowing his words and enunciating them carefully to ensure Lee caught every one of them, "With Ms. Michaels staying in that villa, I cannot risk you going in there and drawing them out. They can't see her. She can't see them. Are we clear?"

"Yes."

Anger burned in his belly, but Lee gave his father the affirmation he needed to end the argument, the same argument they had been having over and over for seven years, and stalked away. As he made his way swiftly away from the desk and toward his living quarters, Lee pondered the woman he was about to go meet. She was beautiful. She was sexy. And apparently she had a personality to match. From the moment he first saw her he knew it was different between them. It was just a matter of how different.

Within a half hour, Lee was freshly showered and dressed in the khakis and crisp white shirt that managed to exude his wealth while still maintaining at least some of the island ease. As he approached the villa, he tucked the hem of the shirt into his waistband, knowing Clark would prefer he forgo a little more of the ease than Lee would like.

This was the uncomfortable balance he and his father constantly tried to maintain. At 25 years old and independently wealthier than Clark, it seemed that Lee had no reason to still be at the resort, acting as a second to his father. Reminders of his mother, however, kept him where he was and brought him back on the few occasions he had tried to walk away and start his own life. The way she died and what it did to Clark never fully left Lee's mind, and he felt that until it did, it was his responsibility to keep things just as they were.

Lee felt suddenly nervous as he climbed the few steps to the front porch of the villa. That was a feeling to which he was definitely not accustomed. Whether in the resort or the forest, he was always calm, always in control. Now as he lifted his hand to knock on the door, he found himself struggling to find the right words to say and both wishing his father had never sent him on the errand and silently thanking him for giving him an excuse to stand right where he was in that moment.

He could hear movement inside from the back of the villa and as it got closer to the door, a light illuminated the front windows. The door opened and the beautiful woman from the path looked out at him. At first she appeared startled, then an expression of unsureness and intrigue crossed her face.

"Hello," she said.

Her voice was low and sweet, almost purring even in her confusion. The feeling in his belly removed all doubt of his earlier suspicions. She was more than alluring. She was his.

"Hello," Lee replied.

The woman gave a slight glance from side to side, then looked back at him questioningly.

"Can I help you with something?" she asked.

"Oh! I'm sorry. Hi, I'm Lee Adams."

"Adams? As in Clark Adams?"

"He's my father."

"Oh."

"And you're Ms. Michaels?"

"At least you didn't try to call me Mrs.," the woman muttered.

"Excuse me?"

She shook her head, causing the coppery ponytail at the back of her head to brush against her back.

"Nothing. Um," she stepped back away from the door, "Would you like to come in?"

Lee stepped into the villa and move out of the way to allow her to close the door behind him. In the light of the living room he could look at her better. She had changed clothes since he saw her just a short time before. Now she wore a long black and white dress that skimmed the tops of her feet and scooped low over her full breasts.

"I'm sorry. Did I interrupt something?" he asked.

"No. I was just getting ready to go for a walk along the beach."

"Would you mind if I came along?"

Her eyes met his and he saw them sparkle back at him.

"Not at all," she murmured, and Lee felt his stomach clench.

# Chapter Three: Something in the Water

The gorgeous surfer boy she had seen crossing the path was the son of the resort owner?

More importantly, why was he standing in her villa asking to go for a walk with her?

Jane wasn't sure what bothered her about that, but something about the shift from the sundrenched man who passed her way earlier in the evening to the buttoned-up professional who stood in front of her now asking to accompany her on her walk made her uncomfortable.

But he was most definitely asking to go with her and she was not about to turn that opportunity down. If nothing else it would give her a few minutes to admire him by moonlight, which was not a way she often got to admire men, particularly not ones as hot as this one.

A smile flickered across his face when she agreed to him walking with her and they turned together to step outside. The evening had softened into a warm but breezy night and Jane turned her face up to the sky to enjoy the gentle movement of the air across her skin. Already she was feeling the relaxation of the island, the magic of the tropical blooms and constant whisper of the waves that would ease all of her tension and send her back home at the end of the week calm, collected, and back at a point where it didn't matter quite as much that her choice of male life partner was a gay best friend, a dog, or a lizard.

They started walking down the path in the opposite direction of the main building, Lee walking slightly in front of her as they left the villa behind them. He turned suddenly and led her down toward the place in between the palm trees where he had disappeared earlier. Stepping into the thickly landscaped plants made it briefly darker, but after several feet they emerged onto the sand of the beach.

"It seems that all of those plants take away from the ocean view a bit," she said as she took in the beauty of the ocean swaying and surging beneath a pale moon.

Lee laughed.

"My father says it is to create a sense of solitude and exclusivity in the villas, and that the mystery will lure you to the ocean."

"That sounds more dangerous than I think he intends it to."

Jane stepped out of her sandals and let her feet dip down into the sand. It was soft and silky against her skin, nothing like the coarse, rocky beaches back home. The surface had cooled in the evening breeze, but the further she dug with her toes, the warmer the sand felt. Out of the corner of her eye she could see Lee evaluating her movements and she tilted her face to look at him.

"Does your daddy know you are out so late?" she teased.

"He does. He sent me to check on you."

Jane's heart sank. There it was. The inevitable ending to the perfect situation. Only she would be able to take a romantic walk along a pristine island beach in the moonlight with literally the embodiment of everything she had envisioned and turn it into a painfully embarrassing situation.

"Well you can report back to him that I am just fine, thank you," she said, pulling her feet out of the shallow hole she had burrowed into the sand with them and starting down the beach.

"Ms. Michaels, wait," Lee said, taking a few jogging steps to catch up with her, "He sent me, but I wanted to come."

"Why?" Jane sped up slightly.

"I saw you earlier. I wanted to – Ms. Michaels, please wait."

Jane paused and turned to him.

"Jane," she said with a resigned sigh.

"Jane," he said, his voice sounding slightly relieved, "My father wanted to make sure that everything was ok after the whole incident with Bitsy. Which, by the way, sounds hilarious and you are amazing for putting her in her place, but you didn't hear that from me."

He said the last sentence in a fast, slightly hushed tone as if trying to get it out before anyone else heard what he was saying, and Jane gave a short laugh.

"She's a piece of work. Is that really her name?"

"Bitsy? Yes, unfortunately, that is really her name."

"Like, on her birth certificate someone actually wrote down 'Bitsy' as if that is an actual name that people younger than 80 have?" Jane asked. Lee snickered and nodded. "Well, you are correct. That is unfortunate."

She turned to look fully at him and their eyes met. For a brief moment she felt pulled to him, drawn to him in a way that she had never felt. It went beyond just the attraction she immediately had for him to something strange and inexplicable. She quickly looked away and instead turned her attention to the ocean. In the darkness it rippled deep purple, then crashed to the beach with pale grey foam.

Flashing a smile at Lee and gathering her skirt in her hands, Jane ran down toward the edge of the water, stopping so that the water just swirled around her ankles. The cool sensation flowed through her and she took another step forward so that she was slightly deeper when the waves rolled in.

"You shouldn't get so close to the water," Lee called to her from his position higher on the beach.

"You seemed fairly comfortable with the water earlier," Jane called back to him.

She watched as Lee approached her cautiously.

"I am comfortable with the water, but you shouldn't get so close to the water at night."

Jane giggled and continued along the edge.

"Are the scary waves going to get me?" she asked, turning her back to the water so that she could look at him.

Suddenly she felt something grab at her ankle. She gasped as she felt herself stumble slightly. The feeling passed and she gave a small nervous laugh.

"Come on, Jane. Get away from the water."

The words were barely out of his mouth when Jane felt the tug at her ankle again. It was harder this time and she nearly fell. Lee ran toward her, grabbing onto her arms to steady her and start pulling her away from the water. She fought against whatever was trying to pull her backwards. The pressure suddenly turned to pain and she cried out.

"Get away from her!" Lee said in a voice Jane could only describe as a growl, "Now!"

With one final twinge of pain, the pressure released and Jane collapsed forward into Lee's arms. He pulled her against his chest and led her higher onto the beach.

"What the hell was that?" she gasped, "Did a shark bite me?"

Lee guided her down to sit on the sand and crawled toward her legs.

"You should be much more afraid of what swims in that water at night than you are of sharks," he muttered as he moved her skirt away from her legs to reveal her ankle.

"What do you mean?" she asked.

He stroked her leg where she had felt the pain, his hands gentle against her skin. The touch hurt, but it also spread warmth up her body and through her core.

"You aren't bleeding," he said softly, ignoring her question, "Does it hurt?"

"A little. It is feeling better."

Lee's hand slid further up her calf, applying gentle pressure to the muscle, then returned to the sore place on her ankle.

"Good."

Lee leaned down and brushed his lips against the slowly receding pain. Jane's breath caught in her throat and Lee glanced up at her. They stared at each other in silence for a few seconds before Lee dipped his head and kissed her leg again, pressing his lips to her skin more insistently. His mouth was hot and wet as it traveled from her ankle up her calf to the inside of her knee. Jane squirmed against the sand, trying to withhold the tiny mewling sounds building up in her throat. Lee's hand came to her other leg, stroking up from her ankle until he reached her knee and pressing it away so that she opened her legs against the sand.

Her dress strained against her legs and Lee pushed it up so that it gathered on her thighs, exposing her skin to the cool breeze and his warm breath. Supporting herself with one hand, Jane pushed the other into his hair, burying her fingers in the thick, naturally blond-streaked brown strands. A whimper escaped her throat as he began kissing again. His mouth worked its way up to the inside of her thigh and she felt his tongue slick across her skin.

Suddenly he lunged forward, forcing her back against the sand so that his hips settled between her thighs and his upper body crushed down on her. Jane ran her hands over his rounded shoulders and along the defined muscles of his back. She remembered what they looked like, golden under the sun and shimmering with oil and a fine mist of sweat. Now she wanted to see them under the silver wash of the moon.

Her fingers grasped the hem of his shirt and pulled it out of his waistband. She allowed them just a moment on the warm skin of his back before bringing them to the button at his neck and releasing it. Still not speaking a word, Lee pushed back to allow her access to the rest of the buttons and she worked them quickly, revealing his body beneath. She flattened her palms against his chest and ran them down onto the ripples of his belly. His eyes fluttered closed and Jane relished the look on his face as she explored his body with her fingertips. Lee cupped his hands over her hips, pressing his fingers into her flesh as if bracing himself.

"Come home with me," he whispered, finally breaking the silence.

Not trusting her voice, Jane nodded in response. Lee backed away to stand up and she immediately missing his weight on her. He reached down to take her hand and pulled her off the sand with incredible ease. Lee didn't stop to button his shirt back up, but held her hand and started back up the beach to where she had discarded her shoes. Jane slipped them on as quickly as possible and followed him back through the landscaped barrier between the villa and the beach. Behind her she could hear the waves crashing and a strange, muted splashing that sounded as though something was walking up out of the water.

Jane nearly had to run to keep with Lee's long, deliberate strides. He rushed past her empty villa and up a hill behind it. At the top of the hill he turned, leading her onto a dirt path that wandered away from the main building and a string of villas.

"Where are we going?" she asked breathlessly.

"My house."

"Where is that?"

It felt strange running to this man's house. When he has asked her to come home with him she just assumed there would be a car involved, but now she realized that he must live on the same grounds as the resort.

"Just at the end of this path. Not too much further."

A few moments later the path took a sudden turn behind another hill. When they came around the bend, Jane gasped. She had been expecting a house similar to her villa, something small but comfortable. Instead, Lee's house sprawled before them, melding into the surroundings as if built into the rocky hill itself. Lights hidden among the landscaping cast pools of light onto the stone-paved walkway leading up to the door, accentuating the shadows that hugged close along the sides of the house.

As they walked closer Jane realized it was not just shadows that made the house look like a part of the rocky hill. The sides of the house themselves had been carved out of the rock, blending with the rest of the house so that you could not access the back of the house from the front. It was an unusual design that gave the house the impression of a fortress.

"This is your house?" she asked, still stunned.

"Yes. I designed it myself and had it built for me. Would you like to come inside?"

Jane nodded and Lee led her to the door. He punched a code into the keypad and a click indicated the lock had disengaged. The door swung open under his touch, revealing an interior just as stunning as the outside of the home. Rather than stepping into the foyer that she expected, Jane found herself in what looked like one massive open room. The space was broken up by gatherings of furniture and a dark wood bar that snaked around one corner. A sunken area was in the center of the room; three steps leading down into an octagonal area with a fire pit embedded in the marble floor.

"I want to show you something," Lee said, his voice low.

Still holding her hand, he led her across the enormous marble room. The entire back wall of the room was comprised of windows with a single door in the center. He opened the door and they stepped back out into the night. A loud, rushing sound filled the area and Jane felt a cool mist settle onto her skin.

Lee touched a button on the side of the house and lights suddenly flooded a breathtaking grotto.

"This is why I chose this spot for my house. I have always loved this place. I wanted my house to surround it, protect it so that I could enjoy it whenever I wanted."

Jane's eyes swept the space, taking in the lush flowers, dense ferns and palms, and the gorgeous waterfall that poured down into a crystalline pond below. A narrow stream led away from the pond and disappeared through a crack in the rock wall, leading, Jane assumed, toward the ocean. The stunning beauty of the grotto disappeared, however, when she felt Lee step up behind her and wrap his arms around her waist. She let her eyes close and her head fall back against his shoulder as his mouth touched her neck.

# Chapter Four: The Pack

Jane's body was warm, soft, and compliant beneath his hands. Lee held her close against him, reveling in the lushness of her curves and the pressure of her hips pushing back against him. He kissed along her neck, letting his tongue slide across the curve of her shoulder. Her hands came up around him and grabbed his hips. He felt her pull him harder against her, willing him forward.

Lee complied by taking his hands from the delicious fullness of her hips and using them to untie the strings at the back of her neck. Her dress slid away from her breasts and gathered at the curve of her waist. He filled his hands with them, continuing to let his mouth play along her neck and shoulder. Jane's flesh felt like satin against his and he ran his hands down her body to enjoy more of it. He had longed for her from the minute he saw her, fallen for her as soon as he heard her voice. Now he could barely control himself as he stroked along the ample curves of her stomach and pushed the thin dress down off of her hips.

The black lace of her panties perfectly cradled the swell of her behind and clung to her wide, round hips just tempting him to peel them away. Just as he hooked his fingers in the waistband, however, he heard an ominous howl in the distance. Jane stiffened against him, her head lifting from his shoulder and her hands falling away from his hips.

"Damn it," he muttered under his breath and reached down to pull the dress pooled at her feet back up over Jane's body.

The howl was coming closer, joined this time by others. The hair on the back of his neck stood on end and his ears twitched. He could smell them now, coming closer, the salt water from the ocean clinging to their fur. He knew they could smell her, too, and were coming for her. The pack didn't like when someone escaped their grasp. They swam so quickly and silently that she had never noticed as they glided up behind her, but he had. He saw their eyes glowing above the water and the glow of their teeth as they lunged for her legs. In the darkness it was easy for them to disappear into the waves before she saw them.

They would come for her now, though. The distrust of humans was getting stronger, so strong that Lee remained close to the resort just to keep them back from the guests, and from this father. Bringing Jane here had been a mistake. The fortress he crafted for his home was enough to keep humans at bay, but it did nothing to deter the pack.

"Do as I tell you, ok?" he said, taking Jane's shoulders in his hands.

"What's going on?" she asked, obviously confused by the sudden shift in his demeanor.

Lee spun her around and looked deeply into her eyes.

"Do you trust me?"

"I don't know you."

"You do know me. You felt it the second you looked into my eyes. I know, because I saw it. Do you trust me?"

"Yes."

"Then I need you to do exactly as I say."

The smell was stronger, the sound louder. She shuddered in his hands. They were not far now.

"What's happening, Lee?"

"Go behind the waterfall. The cave will protect you. Stay where you are. No matter what you hear or what you see, you need to stay where you are. Do you understand me?"

Jane looked terrified and confused, but she nodded and he stroked the hair out of her face before giving her a gentle push toward the waterfall. She clambered over the rocks, not bothering to take the path that was an easier but less-direct route. Her hands clasped her dress to her chest and her hair glowed like fire in the moonlight. If it had not been for the fear and anger rolling through his stomach, he would have taken her right then.

Even as he thought this, just as Jane stepped behind the curtain of water pouring from the cliff above them, the pack appeared around the edge of the grotto. Their yellow and green eyes shone in the night and he could smell their breath swirling on the breeze. Now that they had arrived, they were silent. Their pace was languid as they walked down the rocky wall of the grotto without trouble. Lee watched them, identifying each of them as they approached so he know what he was facing.

"Where is she, Lee?" a voice asked from his side as a large silver wolf shifted into his human form.

"Who?"

The human form of Brian scoffed.

"The girl, Lee. The juicy morsel you brought to the beach. We know you brought her back here. For a little taste of paradise, perhaps?'

Lee knew that the fast-moving water of the waterfall would mask Jane's smell but he was still worried about her. She would be no match against the wolves if they decided they would not tolerate her so close to their forest home.

"She is forbidden to you," another voice said as a red wolf became Emery, "Why can't you understand that. We warned you before when you were playing around with that frail-looking thing."

"But he never brought her here," the voice belonging to the third and final wolf argued as he shifted from his taupe wolf to a tall, gangly human.

"Humans and our kind do not mix, Lee," Brian spoke up again, "It has always been that way, and it will always be that way. We had sincerely hoped that you would not inherit your mother's unseemly taste for human lovers, or that if you did, you would remember what happened to her when she refused to come back to the pack when you turned 18."

"Don't talk about my mother," Lee growled, his bones aching as he fought to hold back the shift threatening to change him.

"She brought it upon herself. If she had stayed away from that human, or at least chosen to bring you back to us so we could raise you properly, it never would have happened."

"Stop."

The three young men were circling Lee. No longer fearful, Lee was only angry. He thought of Jane cowering behind the waterfall and fought the shift harder. This was not how she should find out. This was not how he had intended to claim his mate when he finally found her.

"With everything that is happening in the forest, everything the Alpha has told us, how can you engage with them so easily? This one you found really is delicious, though. For a human, that is. Not so breakable. Perhaps I will play with her a bit."

The rage surged inside Lee and he leapt at Brian, shifting in midair to land fully on the man's chest as an enormous black wolf. Brian fought him back and just as Lee bent to bite into his neck, Brian shifted so that his thick fur protected him from Lee's fearsome teeth. A moment later Emery landed on Lee's back, his claws digging into his sides. Lee reared back with a growl and flung the smaller wolf off of him and onto the rocky ground. Jason hit Lee from the side, taking him off guard and sending him crashing over the edge of the pond and into the cold water.

Jane screamed from her hiding place and the sound pushed Lee to fight even harder. He broke through the surface of the water just before Jason, the brief second giving him the upper hand so that he could sink his teeth into the taupe wolf's face as he emerged. Jason yelped and pulled away from Lee. Brian had recovered from Lee's tackle and stood, his eyes flashing as he turned toward the sound of Jane's scream. He started toward the waterfall and Lee jumped onto the edge of the pond to block his path. Possessiveness and anger fueled him as he raised a claw and brought it down across Brian's neck.

The force of the blow knocked Brian back again and Lee could see that the determination to fight was quickly draining from him. Punishing Lee for associating with a human and bringing her so close to their home was not worth withstanding the wrath of a more powerful wolf defending his mate. The three smaller wolves sank away from Lee as he paced across the path, threatening them with a low growl in his throat and his bared teeth.

Finally they climbed back from where they came, disappearing into the darkness. Lee could feel his heart pounding against his ribs. He had never felt such violence bubble up inside him. The moment he saw Jane at the door of her villa he had known she was meant to be his mate and the pure primal instinct that stirred in him far outweighed his efforts toward self-control. He had always struggled between his loyalty to the older, more tolerant members of the pack and the anger he felt toward the younger ones for their aggression and prejudice. Now he cared only about Jane and whether she would be able to accept both sides of him.

# Chapter Five: Division

Jane cowered against the back of the cave, her mind reeling from what she had just witnessed. The constant rush of the water in front of her had prevented her from seeing most of what happened, but she knew she had seen a vicious fight between four massive animals, animals she had seen change into humans and back again.

Their fight had been so loud and now the grotto had fallen silent except for the roar of the water that had become just white noise in the back of her consciousness. She looked around and saw that there was no way to get out of the cave except for past the waterfall the way she came. Finding the courage to climb to her feet, Jane took a step toward the gap. Before she could go any further, however, the enormous black wolf walked under the waterfall.

The water poured across his thick fur, making it shine in the moonlight that broke through. Jane gasped and stepped back. He approached her calmly, but she could see the determination in his eyes. The huge animal came close to her, paused, and then nudged her leg with his head. Jane lowered herself down and the wolf brought his head up to her neck, dragging his tongue across her skin. The feeling was strange, but she didn't move away from it. He licked her again and Jane brought her hands to the dark fur on either side of his neck, letting her eyes close.

As the wolf rubbed his face against her chest, pushing her dress down her breasts again, she could feel the thick fur softening, lessening, and giving way to smooth, warm skin. Suddenly the mouth on her chest was Lee's and his hands were moving across her with intensity. His fingers pressed into her, filling his hands with her flesh, pulling her close to him. Jane whimpered as his teeth grazed her skin, then sank into her nipple just hard enough to create a brief, thrilling jolt of pain.

Overcome by desire for him, Jane pushed the open shirt off of his shoulders and leaned forward to kiss the dip of soft skin between his collarbones. Lee moaned and tilted his head back to enjoy the sensation of her lips against him for a few seconds before she felt him push her back down to the ground so he could pull her dress completely off of her. He paused long enough to look down at her, his eyes grazing across her as if taking in every inch of her. She felt lush, beautiful, and feminine in his gaze, the spread of her hips and the fullness of her thighs feeling desirable and fulfilling to this powerful man that hovered over her.

Lee grasped her damp lace panties and pulled them off, following their progress with his mouth until it settled at the apex of her thighs. Jane writhed against the cool ground, at the same time willing him to go further and wondering if she could keep her composure if he did. When he did, his tongue delving into her wet, waiting folds and flicking across her taut, sensitive pearl, she cried out, arching against him and grabbing onto his hair.

His slow, torturous licks were a sharp contrast to the speed and fever with which he had gotten to this place, but she closed her eyes and savored every second of the sensation. Lee's tongue swirled gently across her, occasionally dipping inside of her until she felt like she was spiraling into oblivion. Just before she lost all control, Lee moved his mouth away from her. Jane started to protest, but quieted when she saw him sit back on his knees and start to unfasten his belt.

The muscles in his arms tensed and moved beneath his gold-tinged skin as he released the buckle, unbuttoned his pants, and drew the zipper down. She could feel his eyes on her face, but her gaze was locked firmly on his body as Lee pushed his pants down over his hips and let them fall to his knees. He pushed her legs further apart and stepped forward on his knees to get out of the pants and kick them aside.

His body was even more breathtaking than she had imagined when she first saw him in only his low-slung board shorts. The V-shaped muscles over his hipbones defined a flat, chiseled stomach, and a trail of dark hair led from his navel down to an erection that made her mouth water. She wanted to reach out and touch him, to wrap her fingers around the gorgeous shaft and feel its strength in her hand, but something in his eyes told her that she would have to wait.

Slowing down again, Lee flattened his palm against her chest and drew it down between her breasts, over her stomach, and back into her core. He stopped just before touching her and gazed down into her eyes.

"You know what I am," he said to her in a low whisper.

Jane nodded.

"Yes."

"Do you believe what your heart told you the first time you saw me?"

Jane's breath came faster and deeper. Her mind could not fully understand it, but in her heart and soul she knew he was the reason she had come to the island, and why she would never be able to go back to her life before now.

"Yes."

Lee looked at her a moment longer as if to confirm the sincerity in her eyes. Then he moved over her, his hands going to either side of her ribs. His movements were like the black wolf, smooth, controlled, and exuding dominance. Still staring into her eyes, he pushed into her. Jane cried out at the feeling of him sinking deeply inside her, stretching her body to accommodate him. Lee silenced the sound by capturing her mouth with his.

Jane opened her lips to his kiss, welcoming his tongue into her mouth. He kissed her slowly, exploring her mouth as he held his body still within her. She brought her hands to his back and tenderly stroked the muscles that were so tense with the control he was exerting. As her body began to relax around him, she bent her knees to draw her legs up by his hips. This sent him deeper and for the first time Lee reacted, closing his eyes and growling in his throat. She had heard that growl before, but knew this time it was not anger, but pleasure that brought the primal sound from him.

Running her fingernails along his back, Jane delved more into the kiss, stroking her tongue across his. Her hands dipped along the muscular curve on his back, then onto his butt. She gripped the firm muscles there, pressing her nails into his skin as she pulled him even harder against him. Seeming to understand the meaning behind her gesture, Lee started to move. His hips rocked steadily, each thrust sending a wave of pleasure over her. The long buildup made the sensations more intense and Jane surrendered herself to them.

Breaking their kiss, Jane gasped his name and dug more deeply with her fingernails. Lee growled again, more loudly this time, and quickened his pace, pounding into her so hard Jane could feel her back scraping across the ground. He began to grunt with each thrust, building greater and greater intensity until Jane felt a final, hard push and he roared with his release. The sound and the feeling of his cock pulsing within her and pouring into her sent Jane crashing over the edge. Her body contracted around him, the muscles through her legs, hips, and stomach tensing so hard it almost hurt before releasing into a series of tremors that clutched him, pulling him in.

Lee collapsed against her and Jane leaned down to lick sweat from his shoulder and kiss along his hair. When they could move again, he helped her to her feet and brought her to the waterfall. They stepped beneath the water, allowing the steam to cool their bodies and wash away the sweat and dirt. His hands moved adoringly over her and he stepped close enough that her breasts and stomach crushed against him.

"You are my mate, now," he whispered against her hair.

Jane sighed, letting her eyes close so she could savor this precious moment. Suddenly she remembered something she had heard during the violent fight earlier.

"Lee?"

"Yes?"

"What did that other man mean when he said that with everything that is going on you shouldn't be with me?"

Lee's eyes darkened and he pulled her up against him, wrapping his arms around her so she felt fully enveloped in him.

"My Alpha says he has heard rumors that there are hunters coming. They are humans who have been seeking out our kind for generations and eliminating them. They completely destroyed another pack from an island not far from here. If they come, there will be a great division among my pack and in my family."

"Your father?"

"He's human, and hates anything involving the wolves, including me sometimes. They killed my mother when she refused to return to the pack when I turned 18. If the hunters come, I will have to decide whether to stay loyal to my father, to join with the members of the pack who would rather leave the forest and try to assimilate with the humans to protect themselves, or join with the wolves who want to wage war."

Jane kissed his chest, shuddering at his words. What had started as just an opportunity to escape to an island for a few days had become so much more. As Lee bent to kiss her, they were suddenly surrounded by the sound of dozens of howls. They tore through the air, overlapping and mixing into a frenzy that seemed loud enough to make the stars shake.

Lee looked up as if he could hear voices in the howls.

"I have to go," he told her, stepping away from her and rushing to put his clothes back on.

"What's wrong?"

"I have to go to the forest. Something is happening."

Jane dropped her dress over her head as she followed him from the cave, crashing into him as she stepped from behind the water without realizing he had stopped in the middle of the path.

"Jane," he said quietly, his voice strained.

"Yes?" Jane asked, following his gaze and finding what had stopped him in his tracks.

A figure in a black hooded cloak stood in the middle of the large marbled room, something large and metallic-looking by his side. Jane realized the glass door in the windowed wall was standing open and she willed it closed, wished she had shut it behind her when the stepped outside. Suddenly the figure noticed them and ran forward, bursting from the house as he lifted the menacing crossbow he held up to his shoulder.

Lee pushed her to the side, back into the cave and toward the gap on the other side of the waterfall.

"Run."

With that final word Lee took several running steps down the rocky path from the waterfall and leapt into the air, shifting back into his majestic black wolf just as the hooded hunter let his arrow fly...

# The Billionaire Wolf Paradise

*Part 2: Mated On The Speedboat*

Table of Contents

Chapter One: Hunted ............................................................................ 37

Chapter Two: Now We Sleep ............................................................... 40

Chapter Three: In the Beginning .......................................................... 43

Chapter Four: Choosing Loyalties ........................................................ 47

Chapter Five: Raising the Pack ............................................................ 52

Chapter Six: The War Room ................................................................ 56

Chapter Seven: Into the Forest ............................................................ 60

Chapter Eight: Walk Beside You .......................................................... 65

# Chapter One: Hunted

This was not the way her island fantasies were supposed to play out. The incredible sex with a gorgeous guy behind a waterfall part was on point, but that guy turning into a wolf and throwing himself into a possible life or death struggle with a very large, very scary man wielding a crossbow had her peaceful island retreat going off the rails a bit.

Jane ran back into the cave, cowering against the rock wall when she heard Lee growl and a thud that sounded frighteningly like his body hitting the rock-embedded path leading from his house to the waterfall.

Run.

It had been his last word to her before shifting into his powerful, majestically beautiful black wolf form and leaping toward the armed hunter crashing into his backyard. She had done as he asked, complying with his command in the way she knew she would always comply with him. After all, she was his mate, destined for him. At least that is what she had gathered through the angels singing and word dissolving in a pink haze that happened right before he sank into her.

There was a loud snarl from outside and the fear overtook her. She touched the wall behind her, running her palms across it as she desperately looked for a way out of the cave. The screams beyond the waterfall shot through her like ice and tears streamed down Jane's cheeks. Her body felt weak and her knees threatened to buckle under her. She heard another grunt just as her fingers dipped into a gap between two rocks.

Digging her fingers deeper, Jane felt the rock closest to her shift. A tug brought it a few inches away from the wall. Jane could hear whimpering behind the waterfall and Lee's voice in her head, telling her he had wanted her since he first saw her, telling her to run. Anger built in her chest and poured out of her in a deep, aggressive roar as she wrenched the rock out of the way and ducked into the tight hallway it revealed.

*Oh, God, I am that girl David yells at through the television screen.*

Jane put her hands on either side of the hallway to feel her way as she ran through the darkness. Her heart was pounding so hard in her chest she could feel it in her throat, and the same anger that made the fake stone move away under her hand pushed her faster down the hallway. She had come this far to find Lee, she was not going to let a wolf hunter take him away from her without a fight.

Well, that wasn't a sentence she ever thought she was going to have to say.

As she followed the hallway, Jane tried to remember the directions the winding path was taking her. She could feel it angling downwards, bringing her deeper under the rocky cliff with each step. It was as if something was drawing her forward, telling her where to go in the darkness. Suddenly a glow appeared at the end of the pathway and she pushed toward it. She could hear water and feel the rush of air around her.

The light grew brighter until the hallway finally opened out into what looked like an underground marina cut into the rock. Torches burned from cast iron cages embedded in the rocks, filling the space with shifting orange light. Ahead of her she saw a sleek blue and white speedboat tied to a post in the rock edge of the water. Her mind flashed to the swimming trunks Lee was wearing the first time she saw him and smiled.

"My mate likes color coordination. I'll have to remember that," she said to herself, then pause, "Mate," she said again and shook her head. "Yeah, that is going to take some getting used to."

Jane lifted her skirt up to her knees and climbed into the boat, releasing the rope around the post and tossing it up onto the rocky edge. She scanned the complicated-looking control panel at the front of the boat and felt the panic creeping up the back of her neck.

"I am from the city. I grew up middle class. I don't know anything about speedboats," she flipped a few switches, but couldn't get the engine going. "Come on," she said, the tears choking in her throat, "Come on," her voice was rising to a scream, "I don't know anything about fucking speedboats!"

Jane slammed her hands against the steering wheel as hard as she could and sobbed. Finally her hand hit a small key. She turned it and the engine revved to life beneath her. Gasping in relief, she gripped the wheel and turned the boat into the channel. Pushing down on the gas pedal as hard as she could, she directed the boat away from the edge and through the torchlight of the chamber.

The boat sped along the water, filling the small space with the roar of the engine, for a few minutes before she saw the wall. A rocky grey expanse suddenly rose ahead of her as if it cut off the channel right in the middle.

"No. No, no, no, no," she said frantically, looking to either side trying to find somewhere to turn.

The wall kept coming and a second before she was sure she would hit it, Jane felt the horrible, sinking feeling of falling. She seemed to come up out of the seat of the boat as it tipped over the edge of a small waterfall she hadn't noticed. As soon as it landed, the boat zipped under a low ledge and out into a lagoon.

Stars sparkled overhead and she drew in deep breaths of fresh air that seemed cooler after the time under the rocks. She strained for sound, for any indication that Lee was alright. A moment later she heard a snarl and turned to look over her shoulder in the direction of the sound. An enormous black wolf jumped from the rocky cliff to her side and Jane's heart leapt. By the time the wolf made it to the boat, he was his human form again and Jane lunged across the boat to gather Lee into a hug.

He kissed her firmly then pushed her gently back in the direction of the steering wheel.

"The boat. Drive the boat, Baby."

Jane felt the boat starting to veer toward the cliff and grabbed onto the wheel.

"Oh, damn, I'm sorry." She looked over at him and saw a bright streak of blood down his neck and shimmering stains on his hands, "Do you want to tell me what's going on?"

"Not right now. Go faster. Go, go, go."

Jane slammed her foot down harder on the gas and felt the boat lurch as it skidded across the surface of the water and zipped further into the lagoon.

## Chapter Two: Now We Sleep

Lee reached over the side of the boat to catch some of the water spraying up from the wake of the boat. It stung as it hit his skin but he couldn't actually keep a hold on any of it. He rubbed his hands together, trying to remove the blood, but only succeeded in spreading it further across his skin and up his arms. His body was shaking with adrenaline, but feeling Jane to his side started to calm him.

They rode in silence until Jane suddenly reached forward and killed the engine. The boat slowed and finally stopped before she turned to him.

"What the hell is going on, Lee?" she asked, turning to him with terror in her eyes, "I usually consider myself a fairly calm and go-with-the-flow type of girl, but this is all a little bit much for me. First you were just a sexy boy walking by my villa, which was delightful and exactly what David said was going to happen, which is frightening, but then we're on the beach, and something tried to grab me from the water, then we're at your house, and things are happening," she took a breath and Lee smiled, reaching over to stroke her cheek.

"Yeah," he said, the fear and anger of the last hour starting to give way to primal instincts toward her.

"Yeah," she replied, "And then there were people, and then wolves, and people that I think are wolves, and then you – and you are certainly a wolf. Then, more things happened."

"Yes, they did," he whispered, sliding across the seat of the boat to kiss her, "And now you are my mate."

"But then you tell me that there are hunters and then a guy shows up with a giant crossbow and you told me to run and," her voice was starting to sound panicked and Lee wrapped his arms around her to calm her.

She folded so perfectly into his arms and he could feel her shaking against him.

"It's ok," he soothed.

"I thought you were dead," she murmured against his chest and Lee cuddled her closer to him.

"I'm fine, Baby."

"This is just so much, Lee. So much. My biggest concern before I came here was how many bathing suits I was going to need and if they would fit in my suitcase – and if I was going to come back to Hudson glowing because David used him in a costume for an impromptu night pride parade with Alfred and Cleo pulling the float."

She sighed as if she realized that she had completely lost control of that train of thought.

"Ok, I don't know who any of those people are."

"Most of them are animals," she stared across the water at the moonlight reflecting on the swells that made the boat sway. "What's going to happen now?"

Her voice was so soft Lee barely heard her. He cradled her against him, the desire to protect her stronger than anything he ever experienced or even expected to experience. Around them the world felt quiet and calm, belying the scene he left in his grotto and the horror he could only imagine was planned for the forest. At that moment, there was nothing he could do. His responsibility was with Jane, guarding his mate and preparing for what was to come.

"Right now, we sleep."

"But the hunters –"

"Sleep. Nothing else is going to happen tonight. That hunter was alone, and trust me when I tell you that he will not be providing any useful information to anyone any time soon. More will come, but for tonight, we're safe. I will protect you."

Lee pushed thoughts of the grotto out of his mind and focused on the rise and fall of Jane's chest against him. Her shaking eased and he lowered them both to the seat so he could wrap himself around her from behind. She nestled back into him, letting the luscious curves of her body fill in the dips and expanses of his so they melded together. His hand intertwined with hers and came to rest over her heart.

"Twenty four hours ago, I didn't know you," she whispered, and Lee touched a kiss to her cheek.

"Now I can't live with you," he whispered back.

Jane sighed and he cradled her, watching her breathe until she fell asleep, and then closed his eyes and finally let himself rest.

The sun was just beginning to rise when Lee felt Jane stir in his arms. She made a sweet cooing sound and wiggled. The movement made her press against him, the sexy swell of her hips grinding back into his lap. He bit his bottom lip to cut off a moan and tried to shift his position to stop some of the friction that was starting to wake up parts of him who seemed to not be aware she was still sleeping.

Jane sighed and stretched again, this time arching forward enough that one of her breasts pressed into his palm. That was an invitation he simply couldn't resist. Lee let her soft, pliant flesh fill his hand and squeezed gently. He touched his mouth to her neck, kissing the graceful slope before her shoulder. She seemed to respond to the pressure, rolling her hips again so that they coaxed the twitch at the front of his pants into a full, surging erection.

Lee moved his hand from her breast to her leg. The long skirt had risen up around her thighs during the night, and he pressed it up further so he could cup his hand around her bare hip. He kissed her neck again, letting the tip of his tongue touch her skin. Jane gasped slightly and he realized that she was awake. He brought his mouth up to her ear and nuzzled it.

"Good morning," he whispered.

Jane smiled and turned partially over so that her hips were still tucked into his but her upper body was twisted to allow her to look up at him. The red and gold light of the sunrise made her hair glow and accentuated the smooth paleness of her skin.

"Good morning," she whispered back, and lifted her head to kiss him.

Lee tucked his hand behind her head to support it so he could kiss her deeply, opening his mouth over hers and tempted her tongue between his lips. Her eyes opened when their kiss ended and immediately fell to the blood on his neck. She sat up sharply and grabbed his hands in hers, turning them over so she could look at the darkened stains on his palms and trails along his wrists and forearms.

He prepared for her questions, for the horror that would come with his answers, but they didn't come. Instead, she pulled his shirt off, dipped it in the water, and began to gently clean his skin. The cool water was soothing and the gesture loving and nurturing, but his ache for her only increased as she gazed at his arm, following the ridges of his veins with her fingertips as she tenderly bathed away the blood.

# Chapter Three: In the Beginning

He was even beautiful with blood running across his skin.

Jane explored his hands and arms carefully to make sure he was not hurt, and when she saw that he wasn't, she realized it was not his blood she was washing away from his skin. Something about this made her shiver and her stomach flutter. Once his hands were clean, Lee tilted his head to show her his blood-streaked neck. She dipped his shirt again and brought the cold, wet fabric to the darkened stains. Here, right beneath the curve of his jaw, she found a long cut.

She drew in a breath and touched her fingertips to the wound.

"You're hurt," she said.

"It's alright. The arrow just grazed me."

Jane continued to bathe his neck until as much of the blood as possible was gone. Resting her hands on his shoulders for leverage, she swept one leg over his lap so that she straddled his hips. She remaining sitting up on her knees as she lowered her mouth to his neck, kissing along the damp skin until she reached the arrow wound. Filled with a sudden primal urge, she let her tongue slip from her mouth so that she could lick the cut.

Lee's hands gripped her hips and she heard a low growl starting in his throat. That growl was becoming familiar and she knew the wolf inside him wanted to get loose. She shook her head at him and flicked one more lick across his neck. He made a gorgeous wolf, but it was not his fur she was interested in right at that moment.

"Not now," she purred, "I need you to stay human for me."

She gasped as Lee increased the pressure on her hips and pulled her down hard on his lap, tilting his pelvis up to meet hers. She felt his hardness nudging into her hot, wet core and wriggled her hips against it, luxuriating in the friction the movement caused.

"For how long?" he asked through teeth gritted with desire and concentration.

Jane rocked her hips against him again and kissed him, sinking her teeth lightly into his bottom lip.

"Keep the wolf inside you long enough that I can have you inside me."

Lee groaned and tilted his mouth to capture hers again, kissing her deeply as Jane reached down to release the button of his pants and ease the zipper down. She felt him lift his hips so that she could slide his pants down over his thighs. He shook his legs until the pants fell to his ankles, then kicked them aside.

"We're out in the middle of the water," Jane said through slightly labored breath.

Lee nodded, tucking his hands under her skirt so that he pushed it further up her thighs with his arms.

"I know. In my private lagoon. Nobody can see us here. Nobody can hear us."

Jane moaned softly and allowed him to pull her dress up her body and over her head. The early morning air was cooler and made her shiver slightly as it brushed against her skin. Once she was bare Lee caught one nipple in his mouth, sucking it as he brought his thumb down between her thighs to tease the taut pearl already swollen and aching. Jane bit her bottom lip and pressed against his hand. The movement caused her to slide against his shaft, nestling it in her core and slipping against it without him actually being inside her.

Panting, Lee grabbed her hip in one hand and his hard, glistening cock with the other. Jane felt him start to lift her, and pressed a hand against his chest to stop him.

"Wait," she said.

He looked up at her with concern in his eyes.

"What's wrong?"

She kissed him, snaking her tongue into his mouth to reassure him, and moved backwards to climb off of his lap. Leaning down, she brought her mouth to his ear and flicked her tongue across the lobe.

"Maybe you can appease your wolf a little," she whispered devilishly, and then stood and turned around.

Jane heard Lee mutter a few creative obscenities when she leaned over the dashboard, presenting herself to him. In a second he was behind her, gripping her hips as he plunged into her. She was slick and ready for him, but the intensity of him filling and stretching her still made her cry out. One hand stroked down her back, bringing shivers along her spine, then Lee leaned forward and touched his tongue to the small of her back, licking up until his torso was stretched across her back and he was gripping the dashboard beside her.

"Good girl," he whispered into her ear and Jane lost the final grasp she had on her control.

Moaning loudly, she arched her back, opening further to welcome the hard, insistent thrusts Lee had begun. She was most certainly not feeling like a good girl as her love, her mate, pounded into her over the dashboard of a speedboat with the first light of morning beginning to shimmer on their skin, and she was loving every second of it.

Pushing deeply inside her and holding his position, Lee dragged his fingernails down her back, then slid his hand around her hip to bring his touch back to her most sensitive spot. Jane whimpered as he swirled his fingertip into her. She closed her eyes to concentrate on the incredible sensation of him buried within her and his hand working its magic between her thighs. Soon she sagged against the dashboard, her sounds becoming frantic as she felt her climax spiraling upward within her. Taking these passionate sounds as his cue, Lee starting moving again, stroking within her progressively faster and harder. She willed her body to hold off until she heard his groans reaching a fevered pitch, then let go, allowing a cry to escape her lips as her body contracted around him. Her walls gripped him intensely, then gave way to rapid tremors that pushed him over the brink.

The euphoric feeling within her only increased as Lee throbbed within her, spilling into her body. She could barely catch her breath and sounds like small sobs joined each gasp. Lee began to move again, gently rocking into her so she could ride him along the last waves of her orgasm. When he finally stopped and carefully withdrew from her, he turned her around and Jane gazed into his eyes. The sunrise reflected in them, making them even more breathtaking than the first time she saw them. She accepted the kiss he touched to her lips, holding him in place with one arm around his neck so she could savor the sweet, sweaty moment as long as possible.

Suddenly she heard crackling from behind her and she jumped forward.

"Lee?" a voice came from the dashboard, sounding frantic, "Lee?"

"Please tell me that your speedboat is not scolding you for having me draped naked across it."

Lee kissed her on the top of her head and squeezed her butt.

"I certainly hope not, because now that I know what it's like, I plan on fucking you senseless in this boat as long as it is operational, and then possibly moving it into one of the spare bedrooms in the house."

"A nautical playroom?"

"I promise to always take very good care of my favorite toy," he murmured, biting her neck playfully.

Jane laughed and arched slightly to stroke her body against his, enjoying the way their sweat made their skin smooth and slippery against each other. Lee seemed to be twitching back to life when she heard the crackling from behind her again.

"Lee? Are you there? I'm serious, answer me!"

"That's my dad," Lee said, as if the voice had just registered.

He grabbed onto the handset of the radio and pressed a button on its side.

"Yes, Dad, I'm here."

"Are you safe?"

"Yes."

"There's been an attack, you need to get to my house right now."

"I know, Dad. A hunter came to my house last night, but I took care of it."

"No, Lee, an attack in the forest. The pack has scattered." Jane listed as Clark took a shaky breath, "It's started."

# Chapter Four: Choosing Loyalties

*Oh, how I wish I was wearing panties right now. Oh, how I wish I was wearing panties right now.*

With the knowledge of an attack and the threat of impending inter-species war, Jane felt she should probably not be all too concerned about her wardrobe choices, but as Lee led her by the hand along a gleaming marble hallway in his father's home all she could think about was her current lack of undergarments and how the white marble floor was likely not accustomed to the type of reflections it was currently making.

They approached a massive dark wood door with metal straps across it and she tried to pull her hand out of Lee's.

"I'm just going to wait out here. You go on ahead in and talk to your daddy. I'll just —" He gave an insistent tug on her hand, "No? I'm going? Alright. You take this whole mate thing very seriously, don't you?"

"Extraordinarily."

Lee turned and smiled at her, but Jane could see the fear and worry in his eyes. He stroked his fingers through her hair and leaned forward for a gentle kiss before pushing through the door. Inside the cavernous room Clark leaned against a heavy-looking desk holding a small bulbous glass filled with amber-colored fluid. As she looked at him, Jane mused that if he had thrown on a red and black smoker jacket he would have the billionaire porn magnate look down. Instead he was wearing a severe black suit and an intense expression. Apparently the line between bunny ranch and war room was rather thin.

"What is she doing here?" Clark demanded as soon as they walked in.

"It's nice to see you, too, Mr. Adams. Have you been taking hospitality lessons from Bitsy?" Jane retorted and Lee squeezed her hand to quiet her.

"She's here with me, Dad."

"She can't be here, Lee. Ms. Michaels, it's really is lovely to see you, but —"

"Jane is staying with me."

Clark turned to his son, placing the glass on the edge of the desk and holding his hands out imploringly.

"Lee, this is not a luau or a clambake. You do not bring a date to war."

He had lowered his voice as if she would somehow not hear the last few words if he whispered them.

"I can actually still hear you," she said, "and I know what's going on, so instead of trying to get rid of me, why don't you drop the 'I am Batman' thing and start figuring out what to do about the attack."

All of the fear, anger, and confusion of the last day had built up inside Jane until she felt like she couldn't contain anything else. She genuinely liked Clark, but at that moment all she cared about was Lee and helping him through whatever lay in front of them. Darkness rolled over Clark's face and he turned to face her, but Jane didn't back down. Lee pulled her closer and wrapped his arm around her waist, holding out a hand toward his father as if to calm him.

"Jane is my mate, Dad," Clark's head snapped toward the words, "which means that wherever I am, Jane will be."

"She's what?" Clark asked in a strained voice.

"She's my mate. I knew it the moment I saw her. We've been together since you sent me to talk to her last night. She was there when some of the pack visited me and when the hunter showed up. She knows everything."

"Are you sure?"

The question was directed at Jane and she rested her forehead briefly against Lee's cheek, pausing a moment to listen to his heartbeat and breath in the scent of his body.

"I have never been more sure of anything. Lee is everything to me, which means that I belong right here. Whatever he needs from me, I'm here to give it to him."

Jane winced slightly, hoping Clark didn't catch the suggestive overtones that spilled out of her mouth before her brain could catch up with her. He nodded, seemingly unfazed, and Jane relaxed.

"Alright. Well, then that should actually make this easier. If you have a mate now, you won't want to join the war."

"I didn't say that," Lee replied and Clark looked stung. "In fact, now that I have Jane, I am more inclined to fight. Being a part of that pack is what made me know as soon as I saw her that she was destined for me. It was the same for Mom and you."

At the mention of Lee's mother, Clark stepped back, dropping his head as he leaned against the desk again.

"I had never felt something so intense as that first moment I saw your mother. She was so beautiful, and I knew right then that we were meant to be together. But I promised that I would take care of you. She gave her life to keep you away from the pack. Why would you want to fight for it?"

"Mom gave her life to keep me with you, not to keep me from the pack. She said I would never understand who I was unless I knew where I came from. She wanted me to know them, but she wanted more for us to be a family."

The air felt tense and electric with the painful emotions passing between the two men. Jane wondered if she would ever truly understand what had happened in the years before she knew Lee, and if she could ever be enough to help him through it. No matter what, she knew she would try.

"So you want to fight?"

"Yes."

"You could stay here, let everything pass, and then rejoin the pack later."

"If there is a pack left. Dad, I can't just hide in here and let my pack get hunted down like animals."

"They are animals, Lee."

As soon as he said it, Clark looked pained.

"Then so am I, and so was Mom, and my children will be, too."

Jane glanced up at him, startled.

"Wait, we would have…."

"Pups, yes," Lee responded as if it were the most obvious thing he had said to her all day.

Jane shook her head quickly, trying to wrap her thoughts around that concept.

"Wow. That's certainly something to think about."

"I want you to be safe. I want to know that the only family I have left in this world is going to be alive tomorrow."

"I understand that. I really do, but this is a decision that I have to make myself."

"Why don't you ask your mate? If you are so convinced that she is what you want in life, why don't you ask her if she wants you waging war against a group of vicious hunters who have already decimated a pack nearly twice the size of the one in the forest."

"What do you think, Jane?"

"I'm going to give birth to...puppies," Jane whispered to herself, staring at the marble floor as if it would help her to make sense of what was going on around her. Suddenly the fact that Lee was speaking to her broke through her thoughts, "I'm sorry. What?"

"What do you think about this war? Do you think Lee should fight, or should he stay here and ride it out?"

Jane looked between the men, then brought her hand tenderly to Lee's face so she could turn it to look at her.

"I think that Lee should do what he needs to do."

Lee kissed her, pressing himself to her as if trying to transfer what he was feeling to her through his body. When they parted, he gazed down at her.

"Will you stay with me?"

"Today?"

"Today, through the war, and every day after."

"Well, I don't think my landlord will allow me to have any more pets in my apartment," Lee laughed softly and she smiled at him, "so I will just have to stay here."

Lee turned to Clark.

"Do you know what happened in the forest?"

"No. All I know is that there was an attack and there were injuries."

"Did the Alpha survive?"

"As far as I know, he did."

"Good. I need to see the pack. I need to find out what happened and if there are any plans. We're going home and have them meet us there. Are you coming with us?"

Clark shook his head.

"No. I'll stay here. I want no part of this war, Lee, but if you insist on fighting, I can't stop you. I will do everything I can to keep everyone at the resort away from the forest."

Clark stepped forward and gathered his son in his arms, crushing him against him. Jane saw him squeeze his eyes closed as if to block tears from falling. When they parted, Lee took her hand and without another word led her back out the way they came.

# Chapter Five: Raising the Pack

Instead of leading her outside, Lee guided Jane through the living room toward a bookshelf against the far wall. He pulled on one of the andirons of the fireplace beside it and the bookshelf pulled away from the wall a few inches.

"Oh, my God. That is just like in 'The Ghost and Mr. Chicken'," Jane said, pointing at the fireplace as he pulled the bookshelf open more and led her behind it into a hallway. "Did you know that?"

Lee pushed a lever on the wall and the bookshelf closed. He took Jane's hand again and started at a brisk pace down the hallway.

"No," he answered.

He knew she was babbling to fill the silence, to work through everything going through her mind, but his head was spinning too much to keep up with her. She fell silent beside him and Lee continued to pull her along, trying to get the thoughts in his head to assemble themselves into some semblance of strategy. He would call for the pack when they made it through the network of tunnels that led from Clark's home to his, but after that he wasn't sure what would happen.

They had forked off of the main hallway into a darker corridor and were stepping past the false rock behind the waterfall when Jane started talking again.

"So, tell me more about these puppies. Are we talking like a litter?"

"I'm just one."

"Ok. But what about the fur situation? Will they be babies and turn into puppies, or puppies and turn into babies? Will they be able to shift by themselves so they can outrun me when I'm trying to give them their bath?"

Lee stopped in the middle of the pathway through the grotto and turned to her, catching her face between his hands both to quiet her and so that he could look directly into her eyes.

"Darling, I love you, but now is not the time. We will have beautiful pups, they will look like us, and occasionally they will be wolves. In order to have those pups, though, we have to survive. Cover your ears."

Jane looked startled as he released her face and she made no move to do as he asked. Lee reached forward and pressed his palms down over her ears. Tilting his face up to the sky, he released a howl. It was not as strong as it would be if he was in wolf form, but that element of the wolf was always there so he could easily communicate with the other members of the pack.

When he finished, he released her ears. She stared at him in silence for a beat, and Lee tried to decipher the look in her eyes.

"I love you, too," she said softly and his stomach jumped.

He realized he had told her he loved her in a completely absent way and it made his heart ache. Taking her face in his hands again, he touched a soft kiss to her lips.

"I'm sorry that's how I said it for the first time. I should have told you in a better way."

"Tell me again," she whispered.

"I love you," he said quietly, "I love you, I love you, I love you. Now come inside so I can show you."

Lee took her hand and started leading her the rest of the way down the path. At the bottom he came to a sudden stop. Jane hit his back and glanced around him. The body of the hunter was still sprawled on the stones of the patio, the stones around it dark from where the blood soaked in around him.

"No, Jane. Don't look," he said, trying to push her back around him.

"Did you do that?" she asked.

"Yes."

"How?"

Her voice was even and controlled.

"I —" he hesitated.

"How, Lee?"

"I tore out his throat."

Lee sighed and again steeled himself for her horror, for her to push away from him and disappear from his life as quickly as she came. He was prepared for the worst, but again she surprised him. Jane took his hand, pressing her palm to his and firmly intertwining their fingers. He felt the gentle but insistent pressure of her leading him forward, guiding him in a wide arc around the body, and in through the glass door.

They walked in silence until they reached the middle of the living room, and then she stopped to turn to him. Her hands came to his shoulders and stroked across them, then down onto his arms. He felt the tension ease out of his muscles beneath her touch and he let his eyes drift closed. Jane applied pressure with her fingertips and pulled him forward so that his body touched hers. She took long, slow breaths and he felt his own rapid breathing begin to settle until it matched her rhythm.

"You did what you had to," she said softly.

"Jane," he began, but felt her finger touch his lips to quiet him.

"Shhh," she said and he felt her reach down and slip her dress off over her head.

Jane lowered herself to her knees in front of him and released Lee's button and zipper. She heard his breath catch in his throat when she dipped her head forward to draw her tongue up the length of his shaft. As it grew harder, she wrapped her fingers around his erection and used just the tip of her tongue to lick beneath the edge of the head. She took a moment to concentrate her attention on the bundle of nerves on the underside. The movements coaxed a groan from deep in his throat and Jane felt one of his hands come around the back of her head to gently guide her. Wanting to distract him, soothe him, and reassure him, she parted her lips and allowed him to push forward into her mouth.

She reveled in the feeling of him sliding across her tongue and slowed her pace so she could feel the ridges and veins that crossed along the velvety skin. His long, deep breath sent a delicious thrill through her body. Moaning appreciatively, she sped up, using her hand and mouth to stroke him as he buried his fingers in her hair and let the breaths pour out of him in uneven gasps. His sounds were becoming rhythmic and higher pitched when growls from the grotto announced the arrival of several members of the pack.

"Lee," a familiar voice called out and Jane peeked around his hip just in time to see Brian coming into the room.

"Shit," Lee grumbled as he struggled to straighten his pants and fasten them.

"Your buddies have got to stop showing up when I'm naked," Jane said, trying to simultaneously keep herself folded in a ball to conceal herself and reach for her dress where she tossed it.

"I'm sorry," Lee muttered and turned to Brian and the four wolves walking into the house.

# Chapter Six: The War Room

Jane curled into the corner of one of the massive couches in the middle of the living room and watched as Lee and the others sat around a low glass table reviewing large maps of the forest. They were all in human form now and Jane was working on coming up with a way to remember them when they shifted. She was accustomed to finding ways to remember clients at work by linking their names to their personality quirks or wardrobe idiosyncrasies, and it was not lost on her how strange it was that she was now trying to remember which was the red wolf and what color Jason would turn into if he got pissed off enough.

As she listened to them she picked up more details about the hunters and the threat they posed to the pack. It was difficult listening to the stories of their cruelty and the horrors they had executed on other packs in the past years. The pack had taken so many precautions to hide their location and stay concealed, none of them understood how the hunters had found them. Regardless, they all knew that however they had found them, the hunters had only one intention.

Jane was watching the waterfall in the grotto when she heard heavy footsteps and a familiar, protesting voice in the foyer.

*Oh, no. Brace yourself. Help is on the way.*

"Boys, boys, settle down," David's voice reached out to Jane as if through a dream.

"Lee, your father says this man was looking for Jane," a large man said from the door.

Jane climbed off of the couch and watched as two other men half-dragged David into the room. He was wearing orange and yellow board shorts, enormous blue sunglasses attached to a string around his neck, and platform flip-flops.

"Janey, I don't think I can quite appreciate the cultural welcoming traditions of this island."

"Let him go. It's fine," Lee said, stepping out of the huddle around the table and coming to Jane's side.

The two men pushed David forward and he made a show of straightening his shorts.

"David, this is Lee," she said, gesturing from David to Lee, "His father owns the resort. Not that it isn't wonderful to see you, but what the hell are you doing here?"

David cocked his hip and gave his very best put-upon face.

"Why, darling bestie to whom I have devoted my life, I am here to have some fun in the sun." He peered over his sunglasses at Lee and licked his lips, "His father owns the resort, huh? Well, then maybe I could have some fun in the son." He laughed, then realized no one was laughing with him, "No? Not a funny moment? What did I miss?"

Jane walked over the David and took his hand, gesturing to Lee to follow them as she led him up the winding staircase to one side. She didn't know where she was going, but figured there would be a room somewhere at the top of the stairs where she could talk to David about the situation in a way that would keep him focused and minimize flight risk.

"Last room on the right," Lee told her from behind her and Jane steered David in that direction.

They turned into a small sitting room decorated in black and red. Jane shot a glance over her shoulder at Lee, who shrugged and smiled.

"David, sit down."

David sat and looked up at her with worry in his expression.

"What's wrong? I know you've only been gone a day, but I missed you and thought if you could have fun on an island retreat all by yourself, you would have extra fun on an island retreat with me."

"I'm sure we would have a blast, but—"

"Did you find a boy?" He glanced over at Lee, "Oh, you found him, didn't you? Damn, girl. He is truly the embodiment of my surfer boy prayers for you."

"I know, right?" Jane said, temporarily slipping into giggles with David and forgetting about the more serious issues at hand.

"Babe," Lee said from behind her and Jane regained her composure.

She walked over to the sofa where David sat and perched next to him.

"The thing is, Lee is not..." she paused, not entirely sure how to continue that sentence, "Lee is not exactly like other guys I have dated."

"I hope he is tremendously better than the other guys you have dated," he quipped, leaning back against the sofa and crossing his legs sassily.

"David, Lee is not just a guy I'm dating. He is my mate."

She smiled affectionately at Lee, but she could see David's mildly traumatized expression out of the corner of her eye.

"That was a little more than you needed to share with me," he said.

"No," Jane sighed, "That's not what I mean. Well, yes, that is what I mean, but that is not what I mean. Lee is..." she trailed off, her hands falling helplessly into her lap.

"Baby, let me help you out a bit," Lee said

A moment later Jane watched David scramble all the way onto the sofa, tucking his legs under him and gripping the back.

"What the –"

His eyes were wild and Jane followed their gaze across the room to where her beautiful black wolf stood. The animal walked slowly toward her and she reached down to stroke his head. He licked her and a flicker of arousal rolled through her. His howl to the other wolves reverberated through her mind and she found herself digging her fingers through his thick, silky fur and biting her lip as she thought about her unfinished business with him from earlier.

David jumped down off the sofa and started toward the door, but Jane leapt forward to intercept him.

"David, wait."

"Wait? Are you fucking serious? I'm not sure if you are aware of this, but your little boytoy over there just turned into a dog. A DOG, Jane. I know I've dated some dogs in my life, but this is just taking it to a whole new level." He pushed past her into the hallway, then stepped back into the room and pointed at Lee, "A DOG."

"He's a wolf," Jane said, struggling to contain the smile that came to her lips as Lee walked around her legs, rubbing against her and ducking his head beneath her skirt.

"In the contextual situation of this conversation, do you really want to get technical with me about species etymology?"

Jane was opening her mouth to respond when one of the men who had brought David into the room, a towering man with dreadlocks down to his shoulders, appeared in the doorway.

"I'm sorry to interrupt, but they wanted me to tell you that the soldiers are coming."

## Chapter Seven: Into the Forest

David looked at the man, then at Jane, back to the man, and finally to Jane.

"Excuse me? Did the luscious mocha latte man who I asked to bring me a pina colada with a side of extra pina when I got here just say 'soldiers'?"

"Thank you, Liam," Lee said and Jane realized he had shifted back to human form beside her.

"Oh, hell no. You didn't choose one of those third-world islands, did you? What did I say? I said, Janey, read the brochure carefully. Didn't I?"

Lee pushed past them and followed Liam out into the hallway and Jane could hear their footsteps thudding down the stairs. She turned and grabbed David's shoulders.

"David, please. I need you to listen to me now, ok? Nod if you are listening to me." David nodded and Jane returned the gesture. "In the last 24 hours I have done and seen things that I never imagined. I also discovered Lee, and he is exactly as I said: my mate. I know you don't understand it right now, but he is my world, and at this moment he and the rest of his pack are preparing to go to war."

David had been fidgeting and muttering to himself unintelligibly, but this stopped him.

"War?"

"There are hunters who are coming after them. One came here last night and apparently more of them attacked the pack in their forest home last night. It is either go to war or let the hunters come and wipe them out."

"Holy shit, Jane," David said, sitting down at the edge of a nearby chair and putting his face in his hands, "Only you."

"I know. I know. Only me. There is only one of me. But if this war doesn't go well, there won't even be that. I don't want to push you away, but you need to understand that this is very serious. If you need to, go home and pretend you didn't see any of this and try to make Hudson glow in the dark..."

"Accomplished."

"Oh, god. Well, if you have other ambitions you want to pursue, that's fine. I will never, ever blame you for saying you just can't take all of this and need to go. Or you can stay. "

"Do you love him?"

"Yes. It doesn't make sense, but yes. I do."

David nodded.

"Then I'll stay." He gave a long-suffering look to Jane, "As long as you keep him nicely leashed up, everything will be fine."

Jane laughed and realized that tears were streaming down her face. Seeing David had released even more of the difficult emotions she held within her and she found herself truly terrified for the first time since she heard Lee tell her to run. David stroked her back comfortingly.

"If we are going to be a part of this, we should probably go downstairs and meet the soldiers."

Jane linked her arm with Lee's and rested her head on his shoulder as they walked out of the room. They walked quickly down the stairs and joined the growing crowd in the living room. Jane peered over one of the men's shoulders at the glass door leading to the grotto and noticed that the body was gone. Blood still stained the patio, but she felt relieved that David would not see that. There were things that lurked in his past that would only come back if he saw the bloodied hunter crumpled on the ground.

By the time Jane found Lee, the map was covered with circles, arrows, and other patterns. She wrapped an arm around his waist and he pulled her into a tight hug.

"We are going into the forest," he said to her. "The attack on the pack in the forest was brutal, but the Alpha is still alive, and there were only a few casualties. These soldiers are from a separate segment of our pack who live a few islands over. They have more experience with fighting than we do and will help us plan our defense."

"I'm going with you," she said into his chest and he pushed her back, holding her by her shoulders so he could look at her.

"No, you and David are going to stay here."

"But I thought I was your mate and that meant where you go, I go."

"You are, but that also means that I do everything in my power to protect you. The forest is much too dangerous for you, especially at night. We are going to go, meet up with the rest of the pack, and start getting organized before the next attack. You stay here until I come home. You are safe here. I sent a little message to the hunters, and they will not be coming back here."

Jane shuddered, imagining that the missing body of the hunter was likely strongly involved in that message. She clung to Lee's shirt, holding him to her for a few more seconds. The late afternoon sun was burning through the glass doors and she thought back to how the sun looked when she first arrived on the island. Suddenly Bitsy, the villa, and her goals of a week of losing herself in the sand seemed so shallow and far away.

"Come home as soon as you can," she said, trying to keep her voice steady, knowing that this was part of her life from now on and that meant staying strong for the man, and the wolf, that she was falling harder for with each passing moment.

"I will," he said, running his fingers through her hair, "And maybe we can get started on that litter you are thinking so much about."

He smiled and Jane laughed, squeezing him a little closer.

"Well, I'm on long-term puppy control, but we can certainly practice."

Lee kissed her deeply, the pressure of his mouth on her taking the laughter from her lips. He stroked her face a final time, and then followed the rest of the pack out of the house.

"Did you just say 'puppy'?" David asked as Jane sat on the sofa and covered her face with her hands.

"I don't even want to talk about it," she said into her palms.


The minutes ticked by slowly, melding into hours that seemed to stretch on endlessly. Jane stepped into a multi-head shower and stood beneath the water, allowing the stinging heat to wash over her and rinse away the last two days. When she finished, she wrapped herself in a plush blue bathrobe she found hanging on the back door and took a deep breath of Lee's scent within the fabric. It was only a hint, as if he wore the robe just for a few minutes at a time, but enough to make her feel like he was cradling her in his arms.

She walked down the stairs back into the living room, but couldn't find David. Pulling the robe around her more tightly, she roamed around the house, glancing into rooms, discovering more and more of the exorbitant wealth that defined his daily life. She thought back to her life at home and the success she had worked so hard to build. Leaving it behind to be with Lee seemed like a bittersweet exchange. Her heart was firmly with him, but she wondered if she would ever really be satisfied just living off of his billions. As she walked into the extravagant kitchen and ran her fingers along the pristine granite countertops, however, she found herself musing that she was more than happy to try on the role of devoted wife. Her marketing skills could always be useful to the resort if she started feeling restless.

A sudden movement in the corner of her eye startled her, and Jane instinctively grabbed one of the large knives out of the block on the counter. She swung it in the direction of the movement and heard David shriek. A second later her arm was twisted behind her back and he was prying the knife from her fingers.

"Ok, seriously, I have had just about enough threats of bodily harm today. I have reached my bizarreness quota and I am going to have to ask you to chill the hell out."

Jane fought to catch her breath as she wrenched herself out of David's grip and turned to face him. He was wearing a tuxedo that was at once too large and too small, straining at his belly but pooling at his ankles and sagging at his shoulders. The tails at the back nearly touched the ground and he had pulled the cummerbund up over his ribs to make sure it closed. He hadn't bothered to add a shirt to the look.

"What are you wearing?" she asked.

"I went exploring while you were washing the dog spit off of you. I really do have to commend you on this most recent acquisition. Not only does he look like about six feet of sex, but he has a fabulous wardrobe."

"I thought you had outlawed the use of the word 'fabulous'."

"Well, when the tiara fits."

"And the tuxedo doesn't?"

Jane leaned her elbows against the counter and rested her forehead into her palms, taking a long breath to try to calm her shaking.

"What's wrong?" David asked, coming to her side.

"Seriously? I want you to think through what's going on here. I have had around 48 hours to get used to the idea that I'm apparently destined to be with a wolf and now his pack is at war. I'm terrified, David. I have never been so scared in my entire life and all you can do is wander around the house playing dress up. It's like you have no idea what's happening around you, or you just don't care."

David stiffened beside her and she immediately felt guilty.

"You, of all people, should know that I am very much aware of what is going on right now and what this all means. But I also know that sitting around here acting scared is not going to help him."

"I know."

There was a beat of tense silence, then David perked back up and gave her a bright smile.

"Then would you care to join me for some more mansion spelunking?"

Jane took his hand and allowed David to guide her out of the kitchen and down a hallway through the cluster of rooms he had most recently discovered.

# Chapter Eight: Walk Beside You

Darkness always fell earlier in the forest and that night it seemed to creep up on Lee in an instant. He had spent enough time there that the trees looked familiar, but the winding of the paths beneath his feet was disorienting as the pack ran, changing directions and occasionally delving off of the walkway and into the trees. The wind ruffled his fur and reminded him of Jane's touch. This pushed him faster, making his feet churn so quickly beneath him that they barely touched the ground.

As they drew closer to the lair, he began to notice signs of the attack. Extinguished fires still smoldered at the edge of the path, filling the air with the acrid smell of drowned embers. Broken tree limbs littered the ground and a streak of red across one trunk made his stomach turn. They didn't stop running until they reached the lair where guards flanked the entrance.

Dried blood matted the fur over the shoulders of one of the guards and the other had torn cloth wrapped tightly around one paw. Anger boiled inside Lee. Being a wolf had always been a part of him, but one that was on the periphery. He had gone about his daily life, only occasionally visiting the forest or interacting with his pack, particularly after his mother was killed. As he got older, however, he found himself drawn more and more into the forest and toward the pack. The threat of attacks only increased his connection them. Now as he stood looking at the aftermath of the first attack, the smell and taste of the hunter's blood still fresh in his mind, he knew that this was the world where he belonged and the family that he would fight to protect.

"Where is the Alpha?" Lee asked, shifting quickly as he approached the guards. The two wolves shook their heads. "He's not in the lair?"

They shook their heads again and Lee let out a frustrated growl. Shifting back into his wolf, he turned back down the path and started into the forest. He needed to find the Alpha, pledge his loyalty to him, and offer whatever help he could. There had already been enough division in the pack and Lee had always hovered just on the edge, refusing to let himself think about the last thing his mother told him. It was time that he stopped hiding and faced his future.

"Jane!"

A strangled scream from the living room brought Jane and David running. They found Clark on his knees in the middle of the floor, blood seeping through his fingers as he held his stomach. Tucking their hands under his arms they pulled him to his feet and helped him over to the sofa.

"Oh my god, Clark, you're hurt," Jane said, pulling his hands away from his stomach to survey the injury.

A long gash curved from the middle of his ribs around to his stomach.

"Call my doctor," Clark gasped, clenching his teeth against the pain, "His number is saved in Lee's phone."

David ran toward the office and Jane crouched down beside Clark to look into his face.

"What happened?"

"The hunters. They sent threats to the resort and I managed to evacuate the guests. I told them that a hurricane was coming and that they would need to leave immediately. The last ones were still on the ferry to the mainland when the hunters swarmed."

"Is this the only place you are hurt?" she asked.

"Yes. I caught the tip of a machete on my way out of the main building."

David came back into the room.

"He's on his way."

Clark nodded and slid further down onto the sofa so he could rest his head back against the arm. He was breathing slowly to control the pain but Jane could see him shaking.

"Do you know when Lee is going to be back?" he asked.

"No, but I do know that I am going in after him."

She started to her feet and Clark reached out to grab her.

"You can't. It is too dangerous."

"Clark, you are human and look what they did to you. I'm not just going to sit in this house and let them slaughter Lee and his pack."

"You don't know what you're in for, Jane."

Jane stood and glared down at him.

"They don't know what they're in for. Curvy girls at my point in life get through challenges by being either a bitch or afraid. Guess which route I'm taking."

"Lee is very lucky."

"Maybe not at this particular moment, but I am going to do everything I can to make sure that he is every day for the rest of his life. David, I'm going to my villa to get dressed. You stay here with Clark until the doctor comes and I will meet you here on my way back through. Are you coming with me into the forest?"

"Of course I am."

Jane nodded and ran from the house, not caring that she ran along the rocks barefoot wearing nothing but Lee's bathrobe. The villa was dark and quiet, but her door was splintered as if somebody kicked it down. She climbed gingerly through the remnants and paused right inside to listen and see if the hunters were still there. Greeted only by silence, she rushed into the bedroom, threw on clothes, and started back toward Lee's house.

Despite the warmth of the night, the eerie chill in the forest was almost palpable. Jane and David crept along a path illuminated by torches positioned on every few trees. They listened into the darkness of the trees, waiting for sounds that might direct them. She wore the only non-beach clothing she had brought with her, a pair of tight black jeans, a black t-shirt, and black boots laced to her ankles, and her hair was tied behind her to keep it out of her face. David had changed out of the tuxedo and replaced it with one of Lee's T-shirts over his own board shorts.

Suddenly from one side they heard what sounded like whispered voices. Jane walked carefully toward them and peered through the trees at a pair of men standing in the darkness, talking. She couldn't hear what they were saying, but their gestures were animated and emotional.

"Jane!" David whispered harshly from behind her.

She turned and saw him in the middle of the path, surrounded by members of the pack. Some were wolves, others human, and two gripped him by the arms.

"Let him go," she said.

"Jane, what are you doing here?" Lee asked, walking around David as the two pack members released him.

"I came for you," she told him.

Lee walked toward her and she stepped forward to meet him, allowing him to gather her into his arms.

"I told you it was too dangerous. I told you to wait at the house."

"That is not what being your mate, your partner, is, Lee. Your father was injured. I was not about to just sit around and worry that that was happening to you, too."

"Dad? Is he ok?"

"The doctor is with him now. He's going to be fine. But he could just as easily not be, and that could happen to you, too. I know you want to protect me, but that doesn't mean keeping me away. I'm not going to walk behind you through life letting you cut down a path for me. I'm going to hold your hand and walk beside you into battle and we will cut it down together."

Lee's mouth crushed down on hers and he held her to him for a long moment. When he released her, he took her hand and started leading her back to the rest of the pack. In the last second before she stepped out of the cover of the trees, she glanced back at the men conversing in the darkness. Having apparently come to the end of their conversation, the two parted, turning their backs on each other to walk in opposite directions.

In the moonlight trickling through the trees Jane could see the glint of a crossbow over the shoulder of one of the men, and the shimmer as the milky beams illuminated the other shifter into an enormous silver wolf...

# The Billionaire Wolf Paradise

*Part 3: Property of The Alpha*

## Table of Contents

Chapter One: The Lair .................................................................................................. 71
Chapter Two: Called to Defend ................................................................................... 74
Chapter Three: Betrayed .............................................................................................. 77
Chapter Four: Secrets ................................................................................................... 80
Chapter Five: Testing Loyalties .................................................................................... 84
Chapter Six: Burn ......................................................................................................... 87
Chapter Seven: Alpha .................................................................................................. 90

# Chapter One: The Lair

*Somehow, Jane did not think she was supposed to see that.*

The image of the massive silver wolf walking away from the hunter in the woods kept replaying through her mind as Jane let Lee take her hand and guide her along with the other wolves down the torch-lined path deeper into the forest. Around her the air was tense with anticipation and the lingering effects of the earlier attacks. She was scared, but at the same time she knew that there was nowhere she would rather be than right there beside Lee. Her thoughts wandered to Clark back at Lee's house and she shuddered.

She knew that the doctor had mended his wounds and said he would be fine, but if the hunters had been that willing to attack a completely human person not even trying to involve himself in the war, how would they respond to the human mate of a wolf interjecting herself with aggression that belied her lack of both experience with warfare and any discernable physical prowess?

The deeper they walked into the forest, the denser the trees got and the less moonlight shined through them. Soon only the torchlight illuminated the path and those were fewer and further between. Ahead of them the path was completely dark. There was a distinct line in the path between the orange glow of the torches and the intense darkness beyond, and as they approached it, the men around her dropped to the ground as one by one they shifted into wolves. Lee's hand fell away from hers and she felt the warmth of his pitch-black fur against her leg as he joined the other members of the pack in his wolf form.

David looked around himself at the wolves walking by his legs, the look on his face telling Jane that her best friend had still not wrapped his mind around the idea that she had not only fallen in love with a wolf, but that they were now part of a war to defend his pack from hunters determined to eradicate them from the island. Jane, on the other hand, had become so used to the wolves that when she looked at Lee in his animal form she could recognize the shift of his muscles and the color of his eyes. With each moment they spent together she became more aware of the primal connection between them; a connection he told her had always been there even though they didn't know each other. It was this connection that brought them together the moment they saw each other, and what would keep her by his side no matter how terrified she was of what may lay ahead in her future.

When they got to the demarcation between the illuminated part of the path and the darkness ahead, Jane hesitated. Lee nudged her forward with his nose against her leg, urging her ahead. She understood that the path was dark to conceal the way to the lair where they were headed, but she didn't have the acute vision of the wolves and the thought of stepping out of the light that guided her filled her with anxiety. David's hand slipped into hers, offering a comforting squeeze that brought her thoughts back into the moment. Resting her other hand into the thick fur around Lee's neck, she took a deep breath and stepped into the darkness.

Jane allowed the feeling of Lee moving beneath her hand to lead her as they moved along the path. The ground beneath her feet was becoming rougher and occasionally she felt branches scratching at her body as the path became less defined and they moved into areas of the forest where humans rarely, if ever, tread. What was likely only minutes, but felt like hours due to her disorientation, later, Jane could see the glimmer of moonlight ahead and the trees began to thin out. Finally they stepped out of the trees and into a large clearing.

Enormous rock formations and the rush of a waterfall somewhere nearby reminded Jane of the grotto behind Lee's mansion, but this place was rougher, more wild than the pristine beauty of that spot that now felt a million miles away. The wolves separated from the tight group they had maintained while walking through the forest and wandered into the open space, some climbing up onto the rocks and others disappearing into small caves tucked among the formations. All of them looked on edge and Jane had the sudden compulsion to make some sort of noise just so she could get rid of the heavy, tense silence hanging over the area.

Beside her she felt David moving and she glanced over at him. He was doing tiny dance steps, keeping all of his movements contained so that he didn't have to move from the spot where he was standing, but moving just enough that she could make them out. He was muttering something and she leaned closer to hear him better.

"...lost in a crowd. And I'm hungry like the wolf," he sang to himself.

*Exactly.*

He realized Jane was watching him and stopped dancing. David gestured at the clearing and the pacing wolves.

"I thought some theme music might brighten the mood a little."

"So that's what you went with?"

"It is always a good time for Duran Duran."

"I cannot argue when you are so infallibly logical."

Lee shifted beside her and Jane turned her attention to him, listening as David broke back into song. She shook her head with affectionately. Only he could turn this situation into the after-intermission number for "David: The Musical".

"Come with me, I want to show you the lair."

He reached for her hand and Jane pointed over her shoulder at David.

"Is he going to be ok out here? Not every member of the pack knows him and he's not exactly an unobtrusive presence."

By this point David had expanded his dance moves to coordinate with the music solo that was going on in his head. His eyes were closed in concentration and he was dancing with abandon along the edge of the clearing. Any one of the wolves could have taken him out with one well-directed pounce and he would never have known what hit him. Jane was fairly sure a few of them had that very plan in mind.

"He'll be fine. It looks like Liam is keeping an eye on him."

Jane glanced over and saw a sleek taupe wolf stretched across a rock, his eyes fixated on David. If a wolf could smile, that one was. Oh, gracious. David's poor mother was just getting around to embracing that her son wasn't going to come home with a nice girl that wasn't Jane. What was going to happen if he came home with a dreadlocked wolf that he met on an ill-fated island vacation-turned-battle-for-survival?

Best Thanksgiving Ever.

Content that David would be safe, Jane allowed Lee to guide her through the clearing to a large rock face on the opposite side. They walked around the corner and came upon an opening that led into a cavern. They walked through a small initial chamber and then through a tight corridor into a larger chamber with a subterranean pond and waterfall. She was really going to have to get used to this whole rock tunnel thing.

Lee opened his arms as if indicating the whole space and smiled.

"Here we are, Home Sweet Cave."

Jane pointed to the waterfall.

"I am sensing a theme among your homes."

Lee shrugged.

"I like waterfalls."

"Well for a man with enough money to literally have anything that you want, you definitely have simple demands." She walked deeper into the cavern, examining the formations that were barely visible with the small amount of light trickling in from the open mouth of the cave in the first chamber, "Uh huh. I can definitely see why you would choose this rather than your obscenely gorgeous mansion."

She gave him a strange look and he laughed, walking toward her and looping his arms around her waist.

"Sometimes a wolf just needs to be in his lair," he explained, "And sometimes that wolf just needs to be in his mate."

Jane tilted her face up to accept the kiss he brought down to her mouth. Lee's lips opened over hers and she welcomed his tongue into her mouth, massaging it with hers as she pressed her body against him. Her hands drifted from the back of his neck down his back to his hips, then smoothed around to begin loosening his belt buckle. Her hand was just slipping down the front of his trunks, her fingertips grazing his erection, when a muffled thud broke their kiss. She looked over at Lee's shoulder in the direction of the sound and gasped, clinging tightly to him.

At the mouth of the chamber was the massive silver wolf.

# Chapter Two: Called to Defend

Jane clutched at the front of Lee's shirt, terror building in her throat. Though he hadn't turned to look at the wolf behind him, Lee was obviously aware of its presence. He rushed to close his pants and turned to face the silver beast.

"Lee, be careful," she said in a hushed voice when he stepped toward him, but quieted when she saw Lee bow his head toward the wolf.

The silver wolf shifted, becoming the tall, thin man with hair almost the color of his fur she had seen talking in the forest.

"Hello, Lee," he said in a low, dignified voice.

"Hello, Alpha," Lee replied.

Jane's chest tightened painfully. The wolf who had been so deeply engaged in conversation with one of the hunters was the Alpha of the pack. This couldn't possibly be a good thing. She reached out to grab Lee's wrist and he smiled over his shoulder at her.

"Lee, I need to talk to you," she whispered, but he ignored her.

"Alpha, I want you to meet my mate, Jane."

The Alpha looked at her with dark, emotionless eyes and stayed silent for a few seconds longer than was comfortable.

"I see you share tastes with your mother," he replied, but then offered the faintest hint of a smile. "It is nice to meet you, Jane."

"You, t –," she began, but the Alpha looked back at Lee.

"Lee, you are needed outside. The pack needs to discuss our strategies if we are called to defend the lair again."

"Yes, Alpha," Lee said and the man walked away, shifting back into his wolf form as he left the chamber.

"What do I call him?"

"What do you mean?"

"I mean, since he was so kind and welcoming and introduced himself so nicely to me."

"He's the Alpha, Jane. It's not the responsibility of his position to be kind and welcoming. It's his position to lead and protect the pack. You'll call him Alpha, just like the rest of us."

Lee was walking toward the opening of the chamber, but Jane stayed in her place.

"But he's not my Alpha," she said, and Lee turned, stalking back to her with such intensity that she felt a sudden flutter of fear.

"He is as long as you are my mate. You are mine, which means that you are part of my pack and he is your Alpha."

Jane stepped back, unsure how to process the sudden anger in Lee's eyes and the aggression in his voice. He saw her reaction and softened, coming forward to gather her in a hug.

"I'm sorry," he whispered against her hair, "You just learn quickly in my world to never question or talk out against the Alpha. He is the leader and the protector, and everyone is expected to show him absolute respect."

He kissed Jane on the nose and started back toward the opening to the cavern.

"I saw him talking to one of the hunters in the woods," she called after him.

Lee stopped and kept his back to her for a second before turning to face her.

"What?" he asked.

Jane started toward him cautiously.

"Right before you found me I saw two men talking in the woods. One of them had a crossbow like the hunter at your house. When they were done talking, the other one shifted into that wolf that was just in here."

"Jane, here are other silver wolves in the pack."

"No, Lee, it was not just a silver wolf. It was that silver wolf. I am absolutely sure of it. They talked for a while and then they just parted ways. Like Moses-style. Just -" she held her hands together in front of her then pulled them apart quickly to mimic the quick departure of the two men from one another.

"Look, I don't know what you saw, but it was not the Alpha. If he encountered one of the hunters in the woods, he would have torn out his throat and laid his body out in the middle of the path leading to the lair. After the attack earlier, he is not going to just have a nice conversation with one of them and walk away."

"Well, I didn't say it was a nice conversation."

"It wasn't him, Jane. Come on. They're waiting for me."

Lee reached for her hand and Jane took it, going over the conversation in the woods again. She knew that that wolf was the same one she had just seen. She could only hope the sinking feeling in her stomach was wrong.

By the time they made it out of the cavern and back into the clearing, it was completely full of wolves. The entire pack had gathered and wolves of all sizes and colors sprawled across the rock formations, sat on the ground, and stood around the edges, their tails twitching tensely. David sat on one of the tall formations, absently stroking the fur of the taupe wolf lying beside him and looking for all the world like he was posing for his album cover.

Jane climbed up to join him as Lee walked toward the Alpha. As he approached, he gestured toward Jane and David. The Alpha nodded and shifted into human form. Following his lead, the rest of the pack shifted, suddenly filling the space with men and a few women. Jane noticed that they did not resemble a family and wondered how this particular pack came to form.

The Alpha began to speak and the murmur of voices through the clearing quieted.

"I know you all have heard that the hunters have come and that there was an attack. We were lucky this time in that we didn't lose any lives, but they will be back. They have been planning this for some time and if we are going to survive, we need to band together."

"But why did you call us all here, Alpha?" a voice asked from the crowd, "Aren't we more vulnerable if all of us are in the same place?"

"Lee offered us his house as headquarters and the resort has been emptied. Why aren't some of us there and others spread throughout the forest? Wouldn't that give us more opportunity to cut them off?"

"The hunters have taken the resort," Jane spoke up before she could catch herself.

"Who is that?" one of the men asked, shifting into wolf form and coming toward her.

"Stop, Matthias," Lee said, "That's Jane. She belongs to me. So does the man beside her."

David put his hand to his chest with a look of shock on his face, then smiled at Jane.

"Did you hear him? He said I belong to him," he whispered happily, then his face dropped slightly, "Wait, that doesn't mean like... I mean, I love you and everything, Darling, but I just don't think I could-" he glanced back at Lee, then back at Jane, nodding, "Who am I kidding? Yes, I could. I get the top, though."

Jane smacked him on his thigh to quiet him and they turned their attention back to the conversation among the pack. Many of the men were arguing about where the pack should be and what they should do about the hunters still coming. The Alpha was standing by, strangely quiet, watching the arguments. Occasionally his eyes flickered to the dark edge of the woods, and then back to the men.

"David," she whispered, hoping only he could hear her, "Look at the Alpha. Watch his eyes." David did as she asked and then looked back at her, a questioning look on his face. She nodded, "Something's not right."

Jane stood quietly and was easing herself down the rock formation on her way toward Lee when a young man stood up several feet in front of her.

"I agree with the Alpha," he said loudly, "I think we should all stay in one place. We're stronger when we're together."

The second he stopped speaking there was a rustle at the edge of the clearing and the Alpha's gaze snapped up. Before Jane could even turn to look, there was the sickening snap of a crossbow and the whir of an arrow cutting through the air. The young man in front of her reared back as the metal tip burrowed into the middle of his spine, and collapsed forward on the ground.

In an instant, there was chaos.

# Chapter Three: Betrayed

*Oh, damn.*

There were times with Jane hated being right, and this was one of them. Around her the pack was shifting into wolf form and scurrying throughout the clearing, growling and snarling so loudly she could feel the sounds in her chest. Arrows flew through the space, tearing through fur and spraying blood across the rocks. Jane threw herself off of the rocks and curled up against them, keeping her eyes on the Alpha.

The only one who had not shifted, the silver-haired man backed into the shadows and was making his way around the formation that led to Lee's cavern. Amid the screams and vicious growls filling the clearing, Jane got to her feet and started toward the Alpha. Her fear was gone. Now she felt only fury. She had taken only a few steps when she heard a strangled cry and felt a strong impact as a heavy weight hit her from one side. Jane fell to the ground, the weight coming down on top of her. As she struggled to roll over she realized that the weight was one of the wolves who had been in Lee's house with them that afternoon.

"No. No, no, no," she said, pushing back to sit up with the wolf draped over her lap.

His breath was ragged and his fur was disappearing as blood streamed from a jagged cut over his heart. Jane looked up at the hunter who stood only feet from her. She opened her mouth to speak, but before she could get even a word out, the taupe wolf tackled the hunter to the ground, his teeth plunging into the man's neck and pulling back to tear the flesh. The hunter lay still on his back, blood pouring from the open wound and mixing with the dirt beneath him.

Liam shifted and looked down at Jane intensely as if gauging her reaction. She said nothing, but continued to stroke the injured man in her lap. He was shifting continuously between wolf and man as if the pain took away his control.

"Help him," Jane said.

Liam scooped the man up and over his shoulders, then ran across the clearing into one of the caves. Jane watched until they disappeared, and then started for the rock formation again. She could hear the Alpha's voice coming from Lee's cavern and she worried he was in there with him alone. Before she got very far she felt a hand grab the back of her shirt and yank her backwards hard enough to take her off of her feet. She hit the ground hard on her hip and cried out at the pain radiating through her body. A boot pounding against her shoulder forced her onto her back.

One of the hunters hovered over her and the fear started to return to her belly. He leered at her, a fine mist of blood across his face making him even more terrifying. Still reeling from the pain of impact, Jane couldn't get away from him before he dropped to his knees in front of her, wiping the back of his hand over his mouth. For a moment she thought about telling him that she was human, thinking that that may dissuade him from hurting her, but she knew it would never separate herself from Lee in that way. She may be human, but her heart belonged to a wolf, which meant that in her soul she would never be able to differentiate between herself and the pack.

"Aren't you luscious," the man said lasciviously and Jane felt sickness roll through her stomach.

His hands came to the ample swell of her hips and Jane felt her defensiveness spike. Her knee came up to dig into the hunter's crotch and he grunted in pain, falling forward.

"I am far too much for you to handle," she hissed at him and started to move out from under him.

The man sat back on his knees and struck her across the cheek with the back of his hand, the sound cracking in her ears impossibly loudly. Stunned, she dropped back against the ground and he was on top of her, his hands clawing at the front of her pants. A second later there was another loud crack and the man collapsed to the side, enabling her to scramble away from him. She looked up and saw David standing over the hunter, a rifle in his hands. Blood on the butt of the gun showed where he hit the man and she could see memories shimmering in his eyes. She threw herself into his arms, both comforting and finding strength in each other.

"Jane!" Lee's voice cut through the buzz of adrenaline in her head and Jane stepped away from David.

Lee was running toward her through the clearing and for the first time she noticed that the battle had ended. Wolves and men littered the ground and the rock formations, and the forest rang with the voices of the hunters retreating from the lair. As soon as he reached them Lee gathered Jane in his arms and covered her face with kisses, washing away tears she hadn't even realized were falling until she was against his chest.

"My god, David," he said breathlessly, "Where did you learn to do that?"

David glanced down at the gun in his hand and then back at Lee as if coming out of a daze.

"I used to be in the Army," he said.

Lee's eyes registered shock.

"Used to be?" Lee asked.

The glazed look faded from David's eyes and some of the sparkle seemed to return. Jane had seen this transition before. She knew the look of those years coming back and then slipping away. He finally looked up and nodded at Lee.

"Yep. That was a somewhat less...progressive time. They might not have asked, but I told—and told—and told." He paused and looked at the gun again, "I guess it's just lucky one of the hunters dropped this. Well, I guess he didn't so much drop it."

He didn't elaborate any further, but shrugged and smiled at Jane. Lee gave a short laugh and grabbed David's head, pulling him forward to press a hard kiss to his forehead. David stumbled back a step when Lee released him, smiling dreamily and smoothing down his hair.

"You know, it's that type of battlefield behavior that put me in the 'used to be' camp."

Jane suddenly felt a moment of panic.

"Lee," she said, grabbing his arm and pulling to get his attention. "The Alpha. He's in your cavern."

A growl rolled in Lee's throat and he reached out to stroke her face tenderly before dropping to the ground in wolf form and starting at a run toward the cavern.

# Chapter Four: Secrets

The blood boiled through Lee's veins and the edge of his vision was red. He ran to the opening of the cave, then slowed as he entered, listening for the sound of the Alpha's voice.

"They didn't know you were coming, I assure you," the Alpha said, his voice sounding strained.

"Then how were they so well prepared? You said that if we came tonight, they would be completely caught off guard and we would be able to end this without any more battles."

"The young wolves were more aggressive than I expected. They are following the leadership of Lee Adams."

There was a pause and Lee crept further through the stone corridor connecting the two chambers. He flattened on the ground and eased forward on his belly until he could see through the entrance to the larger chamber to where the Alpha and a hunter stood in the middle of the room. For a moment, Lee couldn't understand why he would choose to meet in his chamber. He could have brought the hunter to his own lair. Then it occurred to him that that would have made the Alpha himself more vulnerable in the event that his interactions with the hunters didn't go according to plan.

"Lee Adams? You said that he was barely involved with the pack, that he didn't spend much time with them after his mother's death."

"In the last few months he has become much more involved. I think he has started to suspect his lineage."

Curiosity pricked Lee's ears and he slid slightly further forward.

"That's why we needed to get this done now. He will come of age in two weeks and when he does there is nothing that will keep him from finding out who his father really is, or why you actually murdered his mother."

Anger surged within Lee. The hunter's words burned through his mind. What did he mean who is father really was? Or that the Alpha had murdered his father. Lee was told that an enforcer had killed Charlotte according to ancient regulations within the pack even though the Alpha had wanted to keep her alive. Even as the most powerful wolf in the pack, if there was not a council to change the laws, he could not contradict them.

"It will be done. I promise you. This attack scared the pack enough that it will be easier for you now."

"My men retreated and your wolves killed some of my best hunters."

"Do they really matter?" the Alpha asked, taking a slight step forward, "Does it matter if anybody is left but you? Isn't all you care about getting rid of the pack and taking over the resort?"

"I suppose you're right, but I want this war over. I want the wolves gone and I want the resort. More men are coming, but you gave me your word that you would make this happen for me. Remember that I don't look at you with the same reverence that your mangy pack does. You are just another filthy wolf to me. I'll spare you if you cooperate. If you don't, you will just be another of the dead and I will have taken care of you myself."

Lee shifted and climbed to the top of a formation.

"You won't have to worry about that," he yelled into the chamber and both men turned, taking defensive positions, "I will handle him. But I will start with you."

Lee leapt through the air, shifting and baring his teeth before coming down on the hunter. His mouth flooded with blood from the man's throat and he saw the Alpha running in wolf form deeper into the cavern. Leaving the hunter on the ground, Lee started after him. He had the advantage of speed, but the Alpha knew every inch of the caverns just as well as he did, and with his head start he soon disappeared. Lee continued after him briefly, then decided it would be better to reassemble the pack and develop their defenses rather than pursue the Alpha. His time would come.

Lee turned and ran back through the cavern until he burst out into the heavy night air. Jane was standing at the mouth, wringing her hands and pacing, but David seemed to be keeping her back. Lee ran past them, howling into the sky as he went, hoping that they understood. Around the clearing human forms of pack members were picking up the wounded and the dead, trying to make sense of the aftermath of the attack, but he couldn't stop to say anything to them. He could only continue to run, howling into the sky as loudly as his lungs could force, calling the pack to his house.

Behind him he heard the heavy footsteps of Jane and David running after him. They would not be able to keep up, but it was a relief to know that they were coming. He knew that the hunters would not attempt another attack that night. The first had created enough devastation that they would take the time to regroup and rebuild their forces before they issued another attack. This gave the pack time to evaluate what Lee had overheard from the Alpha and change their strategy.

The war was different now and there would be even more divisions within the pack. Loyalties would be tested and relationships torn apart as the other members of the pack had to decide whether they would believe him and fight, or follow the Alpha to their death.

Lee ran as fast as his legs would carry him through the woods, foregoing the path in favor of the shorter, more direct way directly through the trees. Around him he could hear the breaking of branches and the yips and snarls of the other pack members running along with him. He had to trust that Jane was behind him and that David would take care of her until she was back at the house.

He led the pack around to the back of the house and dove into the lagoon, swimming through the dark water toward the hidden back entrance. As he climbed out of the water, he shifted, shaking the water off his hair. Clark was having a difficult enough night without watching the pack come in as wolves.

They moved quickly along the subterranean corridors leading up into the home. No one dared speak, all choosing to stay silent until they were securely in the home and away from any chance of prying ears. When they got into the house he immediately ran upstairs and searched the bedrooms until he found

Clark. His father looked worn and weak tucked into the bed, his rows of tightly wound bandages just visible around his bare chest and stomach above the comforter tucked around him.

"Lee!" Clark exclaimed when he saw him, his eyes brightening when he saw that his son was still alive.

Lee went to the edge of the bed and knelt down beside it, wrapping his hand around Clark's.

"Are you alright?" he asked.

Clark nodded, adjusting the blanket to cover more of the bandages.

"Just a cut. I'll be fine. Are you alright? Where's Jane?"

"I'm fine. She should be here any minute. There was another attack."

"No. What happened?"

"The Alpha was behind it."

"What?"

Clark struggled to sit up, but Lee placed a hand on his shoulder to push him gently back down.

"Dad, I need you to listen to me and I need you to be honest with me. I heard the Alpha talking to one of the hunters. They said that when I came of age I would find out who my father really was and why mom was actually killed. They said the Alpha killed her."

"Oh, no," Clark whispered, his voice sounding pained, "I never wanted to tell you any of this."

"Tell me what?"

"Lee, I love you."

"I love you, too. That's not going to change, no matter what you have to tell me."

"I hope that's true." He took a long, slow breath as if to steady himself, "I'm not your actual father."

The words hit Lee as if he had been physically struck.

"What?" he forced out through a throat that felt like it was closing rapidly.

"Your mother was mated to a wolf before the division. He was killed before you were born."

Lee's mind was reeling. He struggled to comprehend what Clark was saying to him.

"I don't understand. You've always told me stories of being married to mom for years before I was born. How you two grew up near each other and building the resort was your dream."

"I know, Lee. I'm sorry we lied to you, but we had to protect you. You see, your father, the wolf who sired you, was the Alpha."

Lee suddenly felt dizzy and sat down hard. He tucked one hand against his eyes, keeping the other gripping Clark's tightly. No matter what, Clark was his father.

"If that's true, that means..."

His voice trailed off and he felt Clark squeeze his hand.

"Yes. You are the rightful Alpha of this pack. That's why the current Alpha killed your mother and why he has taught the young wolves that she was killed for her association with a human."

"But he has always been kind to me, even trusted me."

"He lured you in so that you would follow him. He has been grooming you for war since you were born. Your mother refused to hand you over to him where he could control you and lead through you. She died protecting you."

"The hunter mentioned wanting the resort. Why would that matter to him so much?"

"Those hunters have come from a long line of hunters wanting to eradicate your kind. They have been hunting down the wolves for centuries. They are the reason that the packs are so sparse now. This island is sacred ground for the wolves, which is exactly why your mother chose it to start the resort. You come from the most powerful pack that has ever existed. Many say your sire was the strongest Alpha there was ever been. Which means that you are destined to lead with strength, power, and determination that could completely topple the power of the hunters and return the wolves to what they used to be. You could reclaim this island for your pack, and become the Alpha of an empire. That is terrifying to the hunters and they want to make sure that they eliminate you before you truly become a threat."

"Why didn't you ever tell me?" Lee asked softly, tears streaming down his face as he thought of his mother and all she sacrificed for him.

"It is an awesome responsibility, Lee. One that you should have had the opportunity to choose for yourself rather than be forced into it by betrayal and bloodshed."

"But you said you knew the Alpha was grooming me for war. If this was how it was going to be no matter what, why didn't you at least give me the chance to prepare myself?"

"I always hoped that things would change. That either the hunters would give up or that you would choose to give up your wolf side and we could leave the island."

"You would leave everything that Mom built and just let my pack wither away? You would just hand over exactly what the hunters wanted?"

Lee stood and released Clark's hand. He could hear his pack below them and he knew now more than ever than he needed to be with them.

# Chapter Five: Testing Loyalties

Jane stepped into the foyer and immediately heard Lee's voice from above her. She looked up and saw him running down the steps toward her. Taking the bottom several steps as fast as she could, she jumped into his open arms and let him gather her to his chest. His heartbeat pounded against her ear and she closed her eyes to listen to the beautiful, soothing rhythm. He kissed the top of her head and her temples, holding her against him so tightly she almost couldn't breathe.

She never wanted to step out of the embrace or to let go of the grip she had on his sweaty shirt. All too soon, however, it came to an end as he pushed back to look into her face. His fingers grazed the bruise she knew was forming where the hunter had hit her and anger flashed in his beautiful eyes.

"I'm fine," she whispered before he could say anything, hoping to comfort him.

He shook his head and wrapped his hand tightly around hers, leading her back down the stairs.

"No, you're not," he said, "but I'm going to make sure that you are from now on."

Lee stalked across the foyer to join the rest of the pack in the expansive living room. They were all talking over each other and Lee couldn't get their attention. Finally he tilted his head back and howled. Jane felt her stomach tremble and squeezed her thighs together slightly. Getting turned on by a wolf's howl was definitely something she never would have thought would happen before this trip. She hoped it was only her mate's howl that had that impact on her, or a vacation to certain states somewhat awkward.

The rest of the pack immediately quieted and turned their attention to him.

"Do we know the extent of the damage yet?" he asked.

"Five dead, ten seriously injured," Liam responded from the sofa.

David had gone to him as soon as they got into the house and Liam was now lying with his head and shoulders in David's lap. She smiled fondly as her treasured friend stroked the man's back and looked down at him with a tenderness Jane had never seen.

"And the hunters?" Lee asked.

"Eleven dead."

A cheer rose up from the pack and Lee held up his hands to quiet them.

"Now is not the time to celebrate."

"Lee's right," another young wolf said, "We need to find the Alpha. No one has seen him since the battle began."

A few dissenting opinions came up and Lee held up a hand again.

"We do not need the Alpha." He looked at Jane and she saw nervousness in his eyes. She smiled at him as comfortably as she could and he turned back to the pack. "You are my pack, my family, and I have something that I need to tell you before we continue forward."

Lee took a breath and relayed everything from what Jane told him about the conversation in the woods, to the conversation he heard, to what he found out from Clark. By the time he stopped talking, the pack was whispering and shifting uncomfortably, some obviously unwilling to believe what they heard. Jane was staring at Lee, her heart pounding in her chest so hard she worried it would escape.

"He's telling the truth," a strained voice came from the steps and everyone turned to see Clark struggling down into the living room. His eyes swept across the people in the room as he approached Lee. "Everything he is saying to you is the absolute truth."

"I realize that most of you don't know me," Jane started, taking a step toward the pack, "But I do know Lee and I –I'm going to have to ask you to stop licking him, David, yes, I can see you."

She turned her head toward the scene she had caught out of the corner of her eye and saw David pause, his tongue still pressed to Liam's shoulder. He looked up at her wide-eyed.

"What? Wolves lick each other don't they?"

"He is a wolf, you are not a wolf."

"But I like him."

"I don't care if you like him. Just because he is a wolf does not mean you get to lick him while I am talking."

Their voices had dropped to loud, bickering whispers and Jane realized the other members of the pack were staring at her.

"I'm sorry," she said, turning her attention back to them, "As I was saying, I know Lee. I know him with my heart, my soul, and everything within me." She looked at Lee affectionately and found him gazing at her with heartbreaking softness in his eyes, "You are where his loyalties lie. If he says what he told you is true, than it is absolutely true, exactly as he said it. You have to trust him."

The pack dissolved in whispers again and Jane felt Lee tuck his hand against her cheek to tilt her face to his.

"I'm so sorry," he whispered, ducking his head forward to nuzzle her nose with his, "I'm so sorry I didn't believe you. I should have listened to you from the beginning."

Jane shook her head and nuzzled against him more insistently.

"Stop," she whispered back, "It's ok. What matters is that we're here now. All we can do is move forward."

Lee looked back at the rest of the pack and she joined his gaze.

"So?" he asked.

The pack fell silent and one of the men stood to face him.

"Tell us what we should do."

Lee nodded.

"Thank you. Now, we may have won tonight, but there will be more hunters. They will continue to send them. We can't just focus on getting rid of those who are already here, but also prepare for those to come."

There was a tense moment of silence and David spoke up in an uncharacteristically calm, steady voice.

"We need to isolate the island and cut off their access to reinforcements and supplies while still being able to bring in what we need. If we can close them off from everything, the psychological impact will weaken them even further so we can take them down."

Lee nodded and Jane reached a hand toward David. He was pushing past unimaginable pain and fear to be a part of this for her, and she needed him close to her. David eased Liam off of his lap and walked toward her, taking her hand and kissing her briefly.

"What do we do?" she asked.

David thought quietly for a moment, then looked up sharply at Clark. He released her hand and walked toward him.

"How many ways are there onto the island?"

"Just the one bridge and the ferry."

"That's it? No back ways or service entrances or anything?"

"No," Clark said, looking to Lee as if for validation of the claim, "That's it. Everyone that comes to or leaves the island has to take the ferry or the bridge. The waterways are private and no boats can get in through the gates without us activating the system."

"Are all of the resort guests gone?"

"Yes," Clark confirmed.

"All of them? You are absolutely sure?"

"Yes," he said again, nodding emphatically.

David nodded back and turned to Jane again.

"Jane, do you remember what you have always told me is the difference between quitting a job and dumping a boyfriend?"

She looked at him quizzically.

"With a job, you always want the option of coming back, so you never burn bridges, but with a boyfriend you want to completely obliterate that option..."

Realization dawned on her and her eyes widened.

"So you let those motherfuckers burn."

# Chapter Six: Burn

Jane grabbed David and hugged him tightly to her chest, a few tears slipping down her cheeks to soak into his shoulder. She pushed him back and toward the door with the same movement.

"Go," she said and he didn't hesitate.

Several of the men chased after him, some carrying weapons they had brought with them from the battlefield. They ran from the house and when they were gone, Jane turned back to Lee. She opened her arms to him and he curled into them, suddenly feeling small in her embrace.

"Come on," she said quietly against his hair and led him across the living room toward the glass doors.

The adrenaline from the battle was dissipating quickly and throughout the living room the pack was sprawling on the floor and across the furniture, drifting to sleep. Some remained human while others shifted, curling around each other as they all offered each other their comfort and protection. Jane hit the light switch on their way out of the house so that the living room went dark to allow the pack a few hours of much-deserved rest.

Lee took a deep breath of the night air as they stepped out of the house, dropping his head back as if trying to let the breeze wash away everything that had already happened that night. Jane pulled him gently, guiding him away from the house and up the path toward the waterfall, then past it and up the rest of the way to the top of the cliff. It was quiet there and she let out a breath she didn't realize she was holding.

Jane tucked herself against Lee's chest and closed her eyes, drawing the scent of him into her lungs and finding peace in the consistency of his heartbeat and the rise and fall of his breath. He turned her in his embrace so that her back was against his chest and his arms were around her waist. From that vantage point she could see around the island and out into the ocean. In front of her in the distance she could see the dark outline of the bridge leading from the mainland to the island and the shape of the ferry docked near the island.

A moment later a shower of flame burst from the beach and Jane realized David and the pack members were shooting fiery arrows into the sky. They made contact with the ferry and the wooden bridge Jane remembered thinking was so quaint when she crossed it on her way to the island. The flames caught and the archers released another wave of fire. Soon the sky filled with the orange glow of the roaring flames and Jane shuddered. That fire was not just keeping other hunters off of the island. It was also keeping them on it. They were sending the clear message that they were not afraid and were more than willing to fight.

Lee's mouth touched her neck and Jane sighed into the feeling. His arms loosened around her waist to allow his hands to slip beneath her shirt and rub across her stomach. She reached back to grip his thighs, holding him closer as he touched her. The adrenaline, fear, and anger of the night, and anticipation of what waited them in the morning, translated into deep, primal need, and she pressed back against him.

His lips traveled along her neck, licking slowly as he mirrored the pace with his hands along her waist and up to her breasts. He cupped his palms over her bra, kneading her through the lace and coaxing her nipples to tighten beneath his touch. She felt his mouth come to her ear and shivered at the feeling of his breath rippling along her neck.

"Let me make love to you," he whispered.

Jane nodded and felt him ease her shirt off over her head and dropped it to the ground. He undressed her slowly, his hands moving across her with incredible tenderness as he gradually exposed her body to the sultry night air. She returned the gesture, carefully unbuttoning his shirt and pushing it off of his shoulders so she could fill her hands with the luscious firmness of his muscles. He dipped his head to catch her mouth in a deep kiss as she brought her hands to his belt and released it. She could feel him stepping out of his shoes as she eased his trunks over his hips. Her hand ran down the length of his erection and a soft, appreciative sound came from her throat.

She surrendered herself completely to him, allowing him to guide her down to her back on the cool, damp grass. The strength and protectiveness of his presence enveloped her, making her feel beautiful, safe, and loved. Lee kissed down her body, taking his time as he worshipped every inch of her. His tongue dipped into her navel and she gasped, arching against him as her desire began to spiral out of control. Finally he brought his body forward to stretch across hers and the tip of his erection touched her opening. Jane drew her knees up to open to him further. The movement caused him to slide in slightly and they both drew in breaths at the sudden, beautiful feeling.

"I love you," Lee said, meeting her eyes as if wanting her to see the sincerity as he looked at her.

She brushed the hair away from his face and traced her fingertips over his lips. He closed his eyes and leaned into the touch, parting his lips so that her fingers would dip briefly into his mouth.

"I love you," she said back.


Lee brought his hips forward slowly, letting himself savor the feeling as he sank deeply into her. Jane's body hugged him closely, shaping to him as if her body was crafted to accommodate him. He kissed her languidly as he stroked within her slowly. Each glide massaged her deeply and intensely, and she moaned softly beneath him, the sounds making him feel powerful as he felt her tremble at his touch. There was no rush to his movements as he made love to her. He allowed to delicious feeling of her body wrapped hot and wet around him erase the rest of the day and strengthen him for what waited in the morning.

Jane pulled her thighs closer to his body, intensifying the pressure of her body on his and he groaned deep in his throat. He quickened his pace and heard her sounds get higher and more rhythmic as he pushed into her faster but with the same control. Soon she cried out beneath him and he felt her contract hard around him. The feeling pushed him over the edge and Lee thrust into her a few hard times before his body tightened and he felt hot streams pouring into her as her spasms milked him.

She clung to him, whimpering with the final waves of her climax and pressing kisses to his face and neck. Lee met her mouth and kissed her softly. He sucked her bottom lip into his mouth and brushed the tip of his tongue along the center of her upper lip.

They lay beneath the stars for a long time after, not speaking but letting their bodies cool and their breath synchronize. Finally he climbed to his feet and helped her up. He took his shirt and slipped her into it, buttoning it up to cover her so that she didn't have to get dressed before they went inside. She looked irresistibly sexy standing in the moonlight in his shirt, the thin cotton just barely covering the lush swell of her butt and straining against her breasts, her hair wild, and her lips swollen and reddened with his kiss.

He stepped into his pants, buttoned them, and gathered the rest of their clothes before linking his fingers with hers and walking quietly with her down the pathway, through the crowded living room, and up into the master suite. They bathed each other tenderly, and then climbed into bed, not bothering to dress again so that they fell asleep with their skin touching and their bodies entangled.

# Chapter Seven: Alpha

For the second day in a row Lee woke before the sun rose. He took a quiet moment to stare at Jane lying beside him. Her coppery hair spread around her head on the pillow and her face was peaceful and beautiful in the early morning darkness. He touched her soft, smooth skin carefully, tracing the curves of her face with his fingertips. She sighed in her sleep, a slight smile curving her full lips as if she could feel him even in her dreams.

Being careful not to wake her, Lee slid from the bed and crossed the room to dress. He picked up his phone from the bedside table as he went, dialing even as he closed the bathroom door behind him. An hour later the quiet still of dawn was broken by the rhythmic chopping sound of propellers. He stepped out onto the balcony off of the bedroom and took a long sip of coffee as he scanned the horizon. Jane came up beside him and wrapped an arm around his waist, tucking her head against his chest just as the fleet of helicopters appeared in the distance. Lee held her close against him, dropping a kiss to the top of her head as sound grew deafening and the helicopters passed over the house, creating a strong current of air that caused her to curl closer against him.

In the living room below them he knew the rest of the pack was waking up to the sound of war.

"Are you alright?" David whispered.

Jane nodded, resting her head back against the rock wall behind her and taking long breaths to calm herself. They crouched in the grotto behind the waterfall. Beside them the hidden door to the underground tunnels connecting Lee's home to Clark's stood slightly open and she could hear screams reverberating against the stone.

"Open the door a little more," she told David and he complied.

Looking down at her arm she noticed blood trickling from her shoulder to her wrist. As she watched it slick across her skin she realized she didn't know whose blood it was or how long it had been there. She winced at the sounds of the screams getting louder, but she stayed still, exactly where Lee had told her to wait.

The sun was just beginning to set but already it felt like years since she stood with Lee and listened to the helicopters bringing supplies, weapons, and more members of the other half of the pack to the island. The bridge had long since collapsed into the waiting sea and the ferry was gone, but around the island flames still burned, engulfing sections of trees and swallowing portions of the resort. Above them the sky was dark with smoke and impending rain.

"How long do we wait?" David asked in a hoarse whisper.

"Until he comes."

Around them the wolves were encircling the forest and the resort, drawing out the hunters. The human men, exhausted and isolated, were falling one by one to the dirt as the wolves descended. Some jumped into the water in an attempt to escape the battle, never noticing the dark, impossibly fast creatures swimming up behind them. The brutal, vicious fight would soon be over, but there was one final stand to be handled, and Jane was the bait. This was the moment her trust in Lee was tested to its absolute limits. She literally placed her life in his hands.

"Thank you for being here with me," she said softly to David, reaching out to hold his hand.

He squeezed back.

"Of course. Where else would I be? Besides who would have thought that I would come here and end up with my very own surfer boy?"

"I don't know if Liam surfs."

"Well, my very own wolf, then. Can you imagine the Halloween costumes? Epic."

They smiled at each other, trying to force away the horror and bring calm and comfort to the moment. Suddenly they heard heavy, ragged breathing from the corridor leading out into the grotto. She pushed on David's hip.

"Go."

"Are you sure?"

"Yes. Follow the plan. I'll be fine."

David got up and ran from behind the waterfall just as the false rock moved the rest of the way open and the enormous silver wolf stepped out into the hidden cave. Jane scrambled to her feet and pressed against the rock wall, not moving her eyes from the disgraced Alpha. Blood streaked through his fur and his tail was matted. He snarled when he saw her, baring sharp, dripping teeth. She did exactly as Lee had told her, staring into the Alpha's eyes to refuse to show his dominance. As long as she did that there was a better chance that he would continue to intimidate her, wanting her to show her fear and submit to him. The moment she relented, he would come to kill her.

Jane took a step along the edge of the wall, moving carefully toward the path leading down further into the grotto. She couldn't hear the screams anymore. The only sound in her ears was the rush of her blood and the Alpha's growls. Finally she got to her appointed spot, took a breath, and looked down.

The Alpha growled loudly and pulled onto its back feet, prepared to maul her, when another animal cry filled the space. Lee leapt through the waterfall, his magnificent body cutting through the water so that it glistened on his black fur and sent a spray across Jane. As soon as he made contact with the Alpha, sending him crashing against the rocks, Jane ran.

David waited at the end of the path, pulling coils of rope out of the greenery where Lee hid them earlier. He glanced up at the waterfall.

"Is he going to be ok?" he asked.

Jane nodded.

"He's going to be fine. He has to be. He's my mate."

David touched her cheek affectionately and they rushed across the grotto to the edge of the small pond at the base of the waterfall. The guttural screams from behind the water tore through Jane, tearing at her as if she as actually on the receiving end of the claws and teeth the two wolves used against each other. She wished for a moment that they would shift so that she could understand them speaking, but then she changed her mind. She didn't know if she could handle hearing what Lee would say to the Alpha, and what the Alpha would say in response.

The fight seemed to go on for hours. Her stomach turned with each cry that she recognized as Lee's and she felt the need to run up the path to him. As if he could hear her thoughts, David rested a hand on her thigh to still her. A moment later there was a roar so loud it seemed to shake the ground around them and the limp body of the silver wolf broke through the waterfall, sailing through the air and then crashing into the pool beneath.

Blood spread in the water beneath him and when his floating turned him in her direction Jane could see that his body was torn open from the base of his tail to the middle of his stomach. David was already wading into the water to pull him out and Jane helped, tugging him onto the paved patio before looking at David for affirmation. He nodded and her and Jane took off running up the path toward the cave.

Lee lay on the ground behind the waterfall, the ground beneath him stained, and his breath rough and shallow. Jane dropped to her knees beside him and pulled him into her arms, running her hands through his fur to find his injuries. They came back soaked in blood. She whispered to him, pleading for him to stay with her, and gradually his fur disappeared so that his human form lay draped in her lap. Cuts covered his arms, chest, and stomach, and there was a bite mark on his neck where the silver wolf had attempted to tear out his throat.

His eyes opened and she felt a sob wrench from her chest.

"Hi," she said and he smiled at her.

"Hey, Baby."

"Are you ok?"

"I will be as soon as I end this."

She helped him to his feet and he ran down the path steadily despite his wounds. When he reached the patio, David stepped back from the silver wolf. He had tied his legs with the rope. Lee reached for the end of the rope that David still help and wrapped it tightly around the wolf's snout. He picked up the wolf and put him over his shoulders, then carried him up the path and onto the cliff. Once there, he tilted his head back and howled.

Within minutes the cliff was crowded with the pack. When they were all there, Lee put his hands underneath the silver wolf's flank and hip and lifted him over his head. The pack yipped and howled in response. Walking to the edge of the cliff, Lee tossed the body over onto the rocks below where the waves from the inlet would eventually claim it and drag it out into the water.

Lee turned back to the pack and howled again, arching back with his chest pressed to the sky and his arms outstretched, his fisted hands causing the muscles through his upper body to strain and pulse. One by one the wolves laid down in front of him. They stretched their front paws out toward him and tucked their heads down between their legs. Some rolled to their backs in the ultimate sign of submission. Jane felt an intense wave of pride and love surge through her as she watched the pack accept him as the Alpha he was always meant to be.

Hours later the celebration in the forest was still going strong. Torches burned around the clearing and the pack danced and played on the rocks. There had been a period of darkness when the battle sounds finally ended and the dead were gathered, but Lee insisted that those that had fallen in the battle would not have wanted the rest of the pack to give up the joy of their victory and their freedom, but would have wanted them to celebrate.

Jane sat beside Lee on the top of the tallest rock formation, gazing down at the revelry. His wounds were dressed and his mood seemed bright. Suddenly, though, his eyes darkened and his head fell back with a sigh of exasperation.

"What? What's wrong?" Jane asked.

"Bitsy," Lee said, pointing across the clearing.

Two of the pack members flanked a terrified-looking Bitsy as they forced her into the clearing.

"Oh, you have got to be kidding me," Jane said.

Lee climbed down from the formation and Bitsy ran forward, prepared to fling herself on him, but he held out his hands to stop her.

"What's going on?"

"We found her in one of the villas," one of the men said.

"Uh-oh," Jane heard David say and glanced down to see him sliding off of Liam's back and onto his feet.

"What did you do, David?"

"I might have met her in the lobby and thought she worked at the resort and asked her to babysit the animals while I came to find you."

He said the words in one fast rush and Jane scrambled down the rocks toward him.

"You brought my pets with you?"

"Well, of course. I know I joked about Alfred taking care of himself and Cleo, and considering recent circumstances I feel the need to apologize for this next statement, but he's a dog, Jane. He needs some human assistance."

"Lee, he just left me in the villa with those creatures and then there was screaming and fire. I hid in the closet all day."

"Oh, no, Honey, that's just not necessary anymore," David said.

Bitsy rolled her eyes at David, then turned her best simpering, damsel-in-distress look at Lee.

"I was so scared. What's going on?"

"Bitsy, why didn't you leave with the rest of the guests?"

"I'm not a guest," she sniffed.

"Yes, you are. You were supposed to leave with them. You need to get off the island, now."

"But I stayed here to be with you," she said, stepping forward to cup his face in her hands.

"You need to leave," Lee said again, brushing her hands away from him.

"But I stayed with a vicious dog, and a wild cat, and a….a green thing!"

"You brought my lizard with you, too?" Jane asked David out of the corner of her mouth.

"Uh-huh. Hudson was my carry-on," he replied.

"Bitsy, I'm sorry you had to go through all of that, and I'm sure that I will think of some sort of explanation that will put your mind at ease at some point in time, but it's time for you to leave."

Jane snickered and Bitsy shot her a scathing look.

"Oh, my god. Are you serious? You again?"

Jane walked toward her and Bitsy stepped in between her and Lee.

"I believe he told you to leave," Jane said calmly and Bitsy rolled her eyes.

"Look, Ms. Michaels –"

Lee cut her off.

"That's Mrs. Adams to you," he said sharply, reaching around to take Jane's hand and pull her over to him.

Jane stared at him, her mouth hanging slightly open as the shock of what he just said registered. Bitsy had much the same look on her face as she evaluated both of them.

"Are you kidding me? Her?"

Bitsy threw her hands up in exasperation and stalked out of the clearing. Jane knew that no one would ever believe her story of her harrowing pet-sitting adventures, and she sincerely hoped she tried to use them a few times in her manipulation repertoire.

"She's delightful," David said when Bitsy disappeared and turned back to Liam.

Jane looked up at Lee.

"Mrs. Adams?" she asked.

He nodded and wrapped his arms around her waist, lowering a kiss to her lips.

"If you'll have me."

"Do wolves get married?" she asked.

"Well, technically we are already married according to the pack," he said with a smile.

"Oh, really?"

"Yes. As soon as I mated you, we were married and you are mine forever."

Jane gave a short laugh and cuddled him closer.

"So I spent my honeymoon in battle watching my mate rip people to shreds?"

"I will give you a better one," he promised.

"I'll babysit the pack while you're gone," David offered, "I already have the dog-cat-lizard thing down. It shouldn't be too hard to just integrate the rest."

Liam laughed and scooped David up, carrying him out of the clearing.

"You aren't going back?" Jane yelled after him.

"Not on your life, Darling," he called back and Jane smiled.

"I guess you're stuck with both of us now," she said to Lee, running her hand along his chest.

"So you will stay with me?" he asked.

"Of course I will. But I want an actual wedding."

"Absolutely."

"And a real honeymoon."

"Definitely."

Jane kissed him deeply, the rested her forehead against his cheek so she could whisper to him without the other pack members hearing her. Her hands stroked down to the front of his pants and started to loosen his belt.

"Now, why don't you come into the cave with me and let me lick your...wounds," she said, then tugged him close and ran the tip of her tongue up his neck, "Alpha."

Lee growled and she jumped, giggling as she ran from him, making her way into the cavern with Lee nipping playfully at her heels.

Printed in Great Britain
by Amazon